AMERICA'S
MOST WANTED
FIFTH-GRADERS

Other Apple paperbacks
you will enjoy:

The Day the Fifth Grade Disappeared
Terri Fields

Spring Break
Peter Lerangis

Help! I'm Trapped in Obedience School
Todd Strasser

The Easter Bunny That Ate My Sister
Dean Marney

AMERICA'S
MOST WANTED
FIFTH-GRADERS

Jan
Lawrence

and

Linda
Raskin

AN
APPLE
PAPERBACK

SCHOLASTIC INC.
New York Toronto London Auckland Sydney

ISBN 0-590-58295-X

12 11 10 9 8 7 6 5 4   1/0

Printed in the U.S.A.   40

First Scholastic printing, January 1997

For my dear father, Austin N. Speer
— L.R.

For my husband Doug and my darling Teddy
— J.L.

Contents

AMERICA'S MOST WANTED FIFTH-GRADERS

1.
It Wasn't My Fault

My brief career as a paperboy ended suddenly one Saturday at seven A.M. when Mrs. Crowley showed up at my door. She was shaking a soggy newspaper right in front of my face.

"Sorry about that ma'am," I said as politely as I could. "Guess I need to work on my side throw."

She was even angrier than the last time. Her voice trembled when she spoke.

"Once again, Robert," she said, "you've managed to start my day on a sour note."

Well, it wasn't my fault she had a fish pond right in the middle of her front yard.

"It won't happen again," I assured her, forcing a smile.

"Well," she said, "I'll see to it that it doesn't." She threw down the newspaper and stormed away.

I knew then that the job was as good as over. I was already on probation for missing two houses last week. Then I came up a little short after collections. I had to use my tip money to make up the difference!

The worst part was that I still needed twenty-two bucks for a Super Soaker 2000 — the Cadillac of squirt guns.

I took the newspaper, walked upstairs to my room, and started thinking about everything. I really needed to talk to Max. Max's real name is Margaret Anne Laramax, but everyone calls her Max for short. We met in the fourth grade. Her last name starts with an "L," so she sat right in front of me.

Anyway, Max is kind of hard to describe. She's kind of like a girl and kind of not. She's tall and skinny but eats more than me and has long blond hair and blue eyes that match the blue jeans she always wears. She's pretty and everything, but we're not boyfriend and girlfriend. Not even close. We're business partners. Eventually, she wants to own her own working farm. I want to be a famous inventor. Maybe someday I'll invent something for Max's farm.

For now we just have this pet-sitting business. We have two regular customers — a grungy parrot, named Pogo, and Mrs. Carson's poodle, Sugar, who's more trouble than she's worth. Pet-sitting is better than my paper route, but we're not making too much money from it. There must be another way to make a few quick bucks. I called Max.

Max said she remembered that Mr. O'Hara, one of our neighbors, had put up a notice on the bulletin board at school. He was looking for someone to help with yard work.

That very afternoon I was back in business. I showed up at Mr. O'Hara's door and told him I was just the guy for the job.

"Hi, Mr. O'Hara," I said. "Do you still need someone to help you with your yard work? I'm great at cutting grass, picking up sticks — I can do just about anything."

Mr. O'Hara's face broke into a big smile. "Fantastic," he replied. "A lot of kids today are afraid of a little hard work. You know, they don't want to get their hands dirty."

Translation: Nobody else wanted the smelly job of shoveling horse manure out of his backyard barn. Nobody else was stupid enough to accept a measly fifty cents for every wheelbarrow filled. But it was too late for me. Before I could back out, I had a shovel in my hand.

For the next two hours I thought, Why should I get stuck doing this alone? Why not get Max to help me?

So after I got home and fumigated myself, I called her up and told her the details of the job. See, Max is the type who can see the good in everything. I couldn't wait to hear her spin on this one.

3

Ready? She gave me some crazy nonsense about if the pioneers could do it, so could we.

So the following Saturday we took turns shoveling and dumping the wheelbarrow. Max didn't seem to notice or mind the smell. By the end of the morning, I couldn't take it a minute longer. That's when I pulled this piece of paper out of my pocket. It was an ad that I'd seen in the Help Wanted section of the newspaper.

"Hey Max," I said, "take a look at this." It read:

NO EXPERIENCE NECESSARY.
WE'RE LOOKING FOR A FEW GOOD
MEN ABLE TO SCOUT OUT OPPOR-
TUNITY. MAKE $5,000 YOUR FIRST
MONTH.
FLEXIBLE HOURS. CALL 555-6118

"Max," I said, "this could mean big money." I thought her eyes would pop right out of her head.

"Hmm, sounds too good to be true," Max said. "But it's worth a call. Do you think we could really make five thousand dollars?"

"Well," I said, "if it says so in the newspaper, it has to be true."

Max squinched up her face because she was thinking so hard. It always makes me laugh when she does that. She looks like a crinkled-up paper bag.

"Think we should call?" she asked.

"Definitely," I replied.

"Who should talk?"

I knew she wanted to be the one to make the call. "I'll make it," I said. After all, I thought, I *did* find the ad.

"Okay," she said. "But I'm getting on the extension. We should go to my house. We have a cordless and another phone in the basement."

"Well, what are we waiting for?" I said. "Let's shovel as fast as we can and then get out of here."

"Wait a minute. Remember we have to take care of Pogo and Sugar. If we don't get over there first, Sugar will do her business all over the kitchen floor."

"Okay," I said. "We'll do Pogo and Sugar on our way to your house. Then we'll make the call."

So we finished shoveling, and collected our two bucks. We got over to Mrs. Rice's house in record time. As usual, Pogo was yapping away when we rushed in.

"Shut up. Shut up," Pogo squawked.

"Shut up yourself," I said. Then I got out the beak oil and rubbed it on his cracked beak.

"You look marvelous," Pogo squawked again.

"Thank you," Max said.

"He was talking to me," I joked.

"You look marvelous," Pogo squawked for the second time.

I said, "You look marvelous, too, Pogo," but believe me, that parrot looked anything but marvelous. Pogo had a crack running down the middle of his beak, his eyes were kind of crossed, and he was missing a big patch of feathers on the top of his head.

Meanwhile, Max cleaned the cage and put in fresh newspaper.

We finished up and ran over to Mrs. Carson's. Sugar growled at Max so I took her out. Max filled up her food bowl and gave her a fresh bowl of water.

Then we put Mrs. Carson's key back under the mat and ran all the way to Max's house to call about the ad.

I picked up the phone and dialed the number. My hands were shaking so much the receiver almost slipped out of my hands. Four rings and nothing happened. I was about to hang up when I heard someone say, "Who's dis?" I expected someone to say "Hello" first, so it threw me off.

"Hello," I said in my deepest voice. "My name is Robert Douglas Lawrence. I'm a Boy Scout and I have eleven merit badges. I'm calling about the job where you can make five thousand dollars your first month."

"Oh, yeah," he replied.

Once he heard about all the badges, he got a little nicer. "What'd you say your name is?"

I cleared my throat again. "Robert Douglas

Lawrence," I repeated. "Oh, and I also have a friend, Margaret Anne Laramax, who wants the job, too. She's a Girl Scout. We kind of work as a team."

"Perfect," he said. "Oh, by the way, how old are you, Robert?"

I don't know what made me say it, since I'm only eleven, but I said, "Fourteen. Max, that's Margaret Anne, is fourteen, too."

Well, you couldn't believe how happy he sounded to have discovered us. He gave out some crazy kind of yell — sort of like yahoo — then said, "This is rich, this is very rich! Hey, Louie, pick up the extension."

I could tell by the heavy breathing that the other man had picked up.

"Robert," the first man said, "could you please repeat for Mr. Louie everything you just told me?"

"Sure." Then I said my name and the stuff about being a Boy Scout and all.

"Impressive, Mr. Lawrence. I'm impressed. Aren't you, Mr. Louie?"

"Very."

"Where are you kids from?" the first man asked.

"We both live in Thornton," I said. "In the north end. We're sort of in the country."

"Very nice area. We can tell you two must have a lot of class. We'd really like to know more about you and your friend."

I almost didn't get to answer because I could hear Max breathing into the telephone, and I didn't want her to get into her twenty questions routine and blow the deal. I jumped in quickly.

"We could come in for an interview after school on Monday," I said. I hoped I wasn't sounding too eager.

"Sure, Mr. Lawrence. Let me give you our address."

I motioned to Max to give me a pencil and paper.

"Go ahead," I said.

"Four-two-three King Street. We're right above Jansen's Funeral Parlor. Be there at four o'clock." And he hung up.

Max and I just looked at each other. We were so excited we jumped up and down.

Once we calmed down we realized that we had to come up with a story to tell our parents about where we would be after school on Monday. This would be no problem for Max since she belonged to every club at school. The Math Club, Save the Whales Club, Save the Chipmunks Club, you name it. But it was a little tougher for me. When I kicked an orange clear across the kitchen floor, the answer came to Max instantly.

"Soccer practice," she said, "that's the ticket for you! Now, how are we going to get to this place?" Max asked.

Good question. Then I thought of my cousin Vinnie. "We could ask my cousin, Vinnie, to drive us. He just got his driver's license, and he started this business. He calls it 'Deals on Wheels.' He gives discount rides to people who need them. I'll call him."

And it was that simple.

2.
The Setup

On Sunday night, I could hardly sleep. I was so excited I even brushed my teeth twice by accident. The next morning I got up early and practiced my smile in the mirror until I heard my dad's alarm go off.

Everything about me seemed wrong. I wished I were taller. I wished that my face weren't covered with one trillion freckles. And most of all I wished I hadn't gotten a haircut last week because my ears looked a lot like Dumbo's.

Suddenly, my mom appeared out of nowhere. I hate it when she sneaks up like that. I let out a scream.

"Boy, are you jumpy today, Rob." She petted the back of my head like I was a dog or something.

"Well, do you have to sneak up on me all the time?"

"I've been calling you for ten minutes. Your breakfast is getting cold," she said.

The last thing I felt like doing right then was to sit down to breakfast with my parents. I knew I'd have to answer a thousand questions about my life and where I was going after school.

It started the moment I sat down.

"Anything going on after school today?" Dad asked.

"Soccer practice," I said. Okay, I knew it was a lie, but I figured he and my mom were going to benefit in the long run, right?

"Soccer practice?" he questioned. "I thought soccer didn't start until spring."

My dad should have been a private investigator. He never stopped asking questions. I had to think fast.

"Yeah, right," I said, "but our coach wants to find out who will be trying out this year. He wants to see what we're made of. Check things out. You know what I mean?"

"Not really," he said. But then his car pool was out front, honking the horn. My dad jumped up so fast he splashed coffee all over his shirt. Suddenly I was yesterday's news.

"Darn," he said. He blotted his tie with a dish towel, kissed my mom, and left.

"Thank goodness," I said under my breath. I hurried to finish my breakfast, but I missed the bus anyway.

"You're late again, Rob," my mom yelled. "Hurry

up and I'll start the car." Before we left, I ran upstairs and got my suit jacket. I rolled it up and stuck it into my book bag.

When I got to my classroom, I spotted Max immediately. You couldn't miss her. She had on some kind of suit jacket and lipstick, and her hair was pulled back in this weird twist. She looked ten years older.

I was late, so Max and I could only give each other a quick look before the bell rang. Mrs. Hunt, our fifth-grade teacher, looked especially mean that day. Her hair was pulled back in a tight little braid. And her eyeballs zipped wildly around the room, searching for someone to yell at.

Max named her "The Iron Lung," which I thought was pretty funny. But right then she looked at me and that definitely wasn't funny.

"Robert. You're late again. Do you have an excuse?"

"Yes, ma'am," I answered.

I knew this was going to take something big.

"Well, I'm waiting." She narrowed her eyes like a snake.

I lowered my head and said quietly, "My grandmother died this morning." I even made a little sniffing sound.

For a moment I thought she bought it.

"Mr. Lawrence," she began. The whole class got really quiet. Everyone knew that when she called you "Mister" you were headed for Mr. Gomez's office. He was the principal of Penn Wood Elementary.

"Mr. Lawrence," she repeated, "your grandmother must be a very remarkable woman. Yes, I believe this is the third time she has died and come back to life since you've been a student in my class."

"Yes, she really is," I replied. Well, I guess that drove her over the edge. She came charging for me. SWISH, SWISH, SWISH. I heard her pants rubbing together as she neared. Then I felt her cold hand on the back of my neck.

I'd never seen her face that red. Then she hissed, "Do you need me to help you find the principal's office or can you find it yourself?"

"I can find it myself," I said.

Max made a face behind her back. Mrs. Hunt scribbled a fast note and pressed it hard into my palm. It said "Mr. Gomez" on the outside.

All I thought about on the way over to Mr. Gomez's office was how I hoped he wouldn't keep me after school. That would really mess up our plan.

I walked through the lobby and into his office. I handed my note to Mrs. Lee, his secretary. She was really nice. She told me once that I reminded her of her own son. She was happy to see me, but she was sad to see me, too. "Robert, are you here again?"

I just nodded and sank down into a cold leather chair, as far away from the front window as I could get. All the kids who walk by try to see who's in there.

"You know, three visits to Mr. Gomez's office and he calls your parents."

Suddenly I felt like my stomach was going to explode.

She rang for Mr. Gomez. "You have a visitor — Robert Lawrence." There was a slight pause, then, "Okay." She hung up.

"He said you can go right in." She kind of patted me on the shoulder like my mother did before my father was about to deliver some horrible punishment.

I walked into his office and sat down in the chair across from his desk.

Actually, Mr. Gomez was a nice man. It seemed like he knew every kid's name in the whole school. If someone raised their hand during an assembly, he always called them by name.

I handed Mr. Gomez the note and he read it.

"Robert," he said as he removed his glasses and rubbed his eyes. "We've been seeing a lot of each other lately."

"Yes, sir."

"Can you tell me what seems to be the problem?"

I wasn't sure what to say. Actually, I didn't really think I had a problem.

"Well, you see, Mr. Gomez, it's really not my fault."

"Mr. Lawrence."

Uh-oh, I thought. Wrong answer.

"It's everyone's responsibility to get to school on time. And what I'm seeing and hearing is that you have a problem with tardiness."

"Yes, sir," I replied.

"Now, is there some good reason why you can't show up at school on time?"

"No, sir."

"Well, I'm afraid I'm going to have to call your parents. We just can't have this continue."

I gulped hard. This is really embarrassing, but when I thought about him wrecking my plans and losing my opportunity to make five thousand dollars, I started to cry. Right there in his office.

He must have felt sorry for me or something because he got up out of his chair and put his arm around my shoulder.

"Robert," he asked, "are you having some kind of trouble at home?"

I don't know what made me do it, but I nodded my head yes.

"Do you want to tell me about it?"

I shook my head no.

"Is it something to do with your parents?"

I nodded.

"Are they having problems?"

I nodded again.

15

"Are they getting divorced?"

Desperate, I nodded again.

"Well," he said, "I'm not going to call your parents right now. But I do ask that you have a nice long talk with Mr. Wellborn, our guidance counselor. I'm sure you'll find him really helpful. Okay, pal?"

I jumped for joy inside, but for some strange reason I cried even harder. Maybe it was because I was so happy I wouldn't have to stay after school.

"I'm sure it feels good to get it off your chest," he said.

He jotted down a little note and handed it to me.

"Here, Robert," he said, "give this to Mrs. Hunt for me."

He put his arm around my shoulder and steered me toward the door. "Things are going to work out, son. You'll see."

I walked back into my classroom and handed Mrs. Hunt the note. She opened it and read it. Suddenly, it was like an alien had entered her body and taken over her personality. Mrs. Hunt started to speak to me in this voice that sounded like Mr. Rogers, if he were a she.

"Robert, dear, if you could turn your math book to page thirty-two, you can join the class."

All I thought about when Max and I locked eyes was, *This is going to be our lucky day.*

3.
Mr. Louie
and Mr. Lloyd

The bell went off at three-fifteen. Max and I shot out of the classroom like rubber bands.

The plan was to meet my cousin, Vinnie, in the school parking lot. We waited and waited. I looked at my watch. Three-thirty. No sign of Vinnie.

Max seemed irritated. She stuffed two Hostess Twinkies in her mouth at the same time. Max's mom always yelled at her for eating junk because it ruins her appetite for dinner. She eats it anyway.

We heard Vinnie coming before we actually saw his car — if you could call it that. It looked like it might have started out to be black, but it was pretty old. He had painted these two red stripes on the hood to make it look like fire, and the back wheels were so big it looked like the car was jacked up. He had this sign taped to the back window that said DEALS ON WHEELS 75¢ A BLOCK. He screeched up to the curb.

17

"Are you guys going to get in or what?" Vinnie yelled.

We climbed in and I introduced Max. Vinnie didn't bother to say anything like "hi."

"Long time, no see, *amigo*," he said. Then he turned around and gave Max a long look. This was his idea of a joke because we just saw each other at my grandfather's sixty-fifth birthday party.

"Well, where to, squirts?" Vinnie asked.

"Four-two-three North King Street," I said.

"That's a long haul. I usually charge seventy-five cents a block, as you know, but because we're related I'll give you a deal. A flat rate of six bucks."

I just looked at Max. You didn't have to be a math genius to figure out that was equal to twelve barrels of shoveled horse manure.

"How much money do you have on you?" Max asked.

I checked inside my book bag. Sometimes my mom sticks extra money in there for me to buy ice cream on Wednesdays. I counted my change. One dollar and forty-three cents. Max came up with three dollars.

"We have four dollars and forty-three cents," I announced.

"Sorry, guys. You're one dollar and fifty-seven cents short," Vinnie sneered.

"Wait," I said, "how about if we give you another two bucks on Friday?" I figured, we would be rolling in money by then.

"Well, okay. But only because we're close relations. Passengers, prepare for blastoff," Vinnie said. And we were on our way, squealing away from the school.

A few minutes later, Vinnie screeched up to the curb at 423 North King. He turned around and laughed. "My driving's kind of a once-in-a-lifetime experience, huh?"

Too stunned to speak, we gave him all our money and got out.

"He's not exactly a cousin," I said. "He's a cousin by marriage so it doesn't really count."

"Don't worry. We've got bigger things on our mind than that greaseball," Max said.

Max combed her hair and then passed the comb to me. "We want to make a good impression. Here goes nothing," she said.

I had to admit that the building wasn't what I expected. But I figured you can't always tell from the outside, right? Maybe it just needed a new coat of paint, some new windows, a new front door . . .

"After you," I said to Max, and did my butler bow. Max started toward the front door.

We walked in and up a long flight of stairs that led to another flight of stairs. Finally we came to a doorway.

"Act confident," Max whispered to me as I knocked on the door.

The door opened just a crack. I saw that a chain held it. There was no face, but someone asked harshly, "What do you want?"

"I'm Robert Douglas Lawrence," I said, "and this is Margaret Anne Laramax. We're here for the job. Remember?"

Those were the magic words. The door opened fast and we were practically pulled inside.

Max looked scared for the first time ever. Her eyes were darting everywhere, taking it all in. "I'll do the talking," I told her.

"Mr. Louie," the man at the door yelled, "the new employees have arrived." It was as if we already had the job!

When Mr. Louie walked out, I stuck out my hand to shake his. I gripped it hard and I could tell he was impressed. He kind of shook his fingers in the air and said, "What a grip!"

"Excuse the mess," Mr. Louie said. "We're in the process of what ya call renovatin'."

"Hey," I said, "it's not like there're rats running around or anything." But then I thought I saw something dart behind the couch. Probably just a pet hamster that got loose.

Mr. Louie thought I was a pretty funny guy. He laughed after everything I said. I had to admit he didn't look like a millionaire. But I figured he must be a really busy man and didn't have time to go to the dentist. One of his front teeth was missing. He was dressed pretty sloppy for a businessman. In fact, his undershirt hung out from his pants.

But as my dad always says, "When you're really rich, you don't have to flash it."

Mr. Louie pointed to the couch. "Sit down. I see that you've met my partner, Mr. Lloyd."

Mr. Lloyd was the one who had answered the door. It was pretty clear by looking at him that Mr. Louie was the brains of the operation. Mr. Lloyd had one of those shaven cue ball heads and two gold teeth in front. I had to admit he was a little strange-looking.

Max and I shook his hand, too. Afterward, I noticed my hand smelled like onions. We sat back down.

Mr. Louie spoke first. "So what makes you guys think you'd be right for the job?"

I jumped in first.

"Well, as I told you, we're both Scouts . . ." They raised their eyebrows. They were definitely impressed.

"I'm a Boy Scout, Troop two-two-four."

"And I'm a Girl Scout and honor student. Plus, Robert and I have our own business," Max said proudly.

"Actually," I said, "Max and I have been running a pet-sitting business for over a year now. It's pretty successful."

Mr. Louie looked interested, so I kept going.

"In fact," I added, "one of our customers trusts us with her very, very valuable prize parrot. It came all the way from Africa."

"No kidding," Mr. Louie said. "What would ya pay for an item like that?"

"Ten thousand dollars," I said. "Or more."

Max threw me a funny look because we always talked about how old and grungy Pogo was. I ignored her.

"It's the only parrot in the world that says 'Shut up' and 'You look marvelous.' It sounds just like a real person."

"Very interesting," Mr. Louie said. "I'll keep that in mind."

"Now," Mr. Louie said, "do you two want to make some serious money?"

We nodded.

"Are you willing to work hard and take an oath of secrecy?"

We nodded again.

"Good. Because if anyone finds out, they'll want a piece of the action."

Then all four of us put our hands together and repeated the secrecy oath.

"Now, let's see if you guys can pass the test," Mr. Louie said. "This is where we separate the men from the boys, and the girls," he winked at Max.

My palms started to sweat. I heard Max gulp.

"Okay, Scouts?" He gave a little laugh. "There

are those that are rich and those that are poor. Know where I'm coming from?"

He didn't give me time to answer. He just kept talking.

"You wanna have bucks, you gotta know people with bucks. You get what I'm talking about?"

We both nodded.

Mr. Louie and Mr. Lloyd looked at each other, and I couldn't believe it but Mr. Louie said, "This is a winning team."

My heart felt like a bottle of soda that had been shaken up with the lid on. I thought it would explode with happiness.

"Are you saying we've got the job?" I said.

"Robert," Mr. Louie said, "let me just say that Mr. Lloyd and myself have interviewed thousands of applicants."

"Never before have we been more impressed or more certain that we have found the right two for the job. It's no wonder you and Max are partners."

Max and I slapped each other a high five.

It was then I realized we didn't know exactly what the job was. I hoped I didn't seem too stupid asking, but I asked anyway.

"Um," I said, "could you tell me exactly what the job is and how we can earn five thousand dollars in the first month?"

Mr. Louie looked me right in the eye. "You know, those are the kind of smart questions that make me sure you can handle this job."

I felt really proud, but I tried not to smirk.

"Well, Mr. Lloyd and I have put together your salesmen's kits. And we have a contract here we'd like you both to sign."

He handed me the contract. It was five pages long. I couldn't really understand what it said. Mr. Lloyd must have seen I was stalling, so he stuck a pen in my hand and just said, "Sign it. All it says is we're partners all the way." I signed it and then Max did, too.

He handed each of us a cardboard box. On the top was handwritten "Cash-in-Advance Cookies."

"Open them," Mr. Louie commanded.

I took off the top, and inside were four boxes of what looked like ordinary cookies you buy at the store.

"The brochures are still at the printers," Mr. Lloyd said. Then he and Mr. Louie started laughing again. They really seemed to enjoy their work.

"What's the plan?" I asked. "Who are our customers?" I wanted them to know I wasn't fooling around.

"Oh, yeah, the plan. Well, you guys already live in our selling district. That's lucky for you so you don't have to drive anywhere."

"Oh, good. Vinnie won't cut into our profits," Max said, looking at me.

"Let me make something very clear, guys. These cookies are very special. They're an old family recipe that can't be duplicated. People go

24

crazy over them. You may not be able to sell them to all the people you know because they always try to push for a discount."

Then Mr. Lloyd sang, "Can't get enough."

"In fact, through our extensive research, we've learned we have a huge customer base throughout the country. We can't import them fast enough."

"Wow," I said.

"But there's a little catch. Nobody can buy this product unless they agree to an in-depth interview. Because once you feel they are good people, they get a box of cookies for only two dollars and ninety-five cents. And we include their name in our grand-prize drawing."

"What's the prize?" I tried to ask but Max interrupted.

"How do we make five thousand dollars the first month if the cookies cost only two dollars and ninety-five cents?" Max asked.

"Very, very good question," Mr. Louie said. "Ever hear of a little organization called the Girl Scouts? Imagine what they rake in. So it's simple. Repeat business. We have found our customers are very loyal, and once they buy one box of cookies from us, we become their source for life. Forget Acme. Forget Girl Scout cookies. See, we pay you on full potential sales calculated annually." I could tell by Max's face that he lost her on that one.

"Just remember, asking questions is the most

important thing. And be sure to write down your answers."

"Everything is extremely confidential. You got it?" Mr. Lloyd said.

I stuck out my hand to shake. I wanted them to know I got it without saying a word. Max did the same.

"We'll meet here every Monday at four."

"Four o'clock next Monday," I said. We picked up our kits, shoved them into our book bags, and left.

There was only one problem. We'd forgotten about how we'd get home. But who wouldn't have with an opportunity like that, right?

4.
Easy Street

Max and I didn't make it home that night by dinnertime. In fact, we didn't even make it home for dessert.

When we left Mr. Louie and Mr. Lloyd's place it was starting to get dark. We didn't have any money left so we just started walking.

All I can say was that it must have been my lucky shark-tooth necklace. After only five minutes of walking, we ran smack into Mr. Ross, our old mailman. He was happy to see us, but he wanted to know what we were doing downtown at night. We said we had a meeting. I was glad he didn't ask too many more questions before he offered us a ride home.

Needless to say, my parents did not look happy when I walked in the door. I felt bad that I made them worry, but I figured that when they saw all that money, they'd understand.

My dad said he was going to call the soccer coach if it ever happened again. Then he got into the whole bit about losing my paper route. My boss, or shall I say my ex-boss, had called before I'd gotten around to mentioning it. My mom had called everyone she knew, but she was so happy to see me that she forgot about being mad.

The next morning, Max wasn't on the bus. I got a little worried and watched the clock. Sure enough, at nine-thirty she showed up with a big smile and a note for Mrs. Hunt.

I think she was the only one in the whole class that Mrs. Hunt really liked. Maybe it was because she knew the answer to every question. Or maybe because she never got into trouble. Until she met me, that is.

So anyway, I tried to catch Max's eye to see if she had gotten in trouble last night, too. But she was already opening her science book. I knew it was no use. I looked over at my friend Jeffrey.

Jeffrey told me once that he was going to ask Max to go out with him. That was a joke since Max didn't act like Jeffrey was alive, except on Wednesdays when he bought her ice cream with his allowance.

Well, anyway, most of the morning I tried to concentrate on my work. I'm really good at science, so I was kind of enjoying it. But every once in a while I thought about our plan and got off track. I couldn't wait until the bell rang for recess so Max and I could talk.

It finally rang, and I jumped out of my seat. But fate had other plans.

"Robert." Mrs. Hunt curled her finger for me to come to her desk.

"You're going to have to skip recess today. Mr. Wellborn would like you to visit with him," she whispered.

Looking back, I can see how Mr. Wellborn got dragged in, how my lie to the principal got me into this mess. But at the time I wasn't really thinking about anything past recess and lunch and planning with Max.

So, while everyone else had fun outside, I had to sit in a chair and wait to talk to a grown-up.

Most kids liked Mr. Wellborn. He was nice to us. I still feel sorry about the whole thing, but here's how it started:

He came out into the waiting room and said, "It's nice to see you, Robert. Come on in." Mr. Wellborn always dressed in really bright clothes, different from the other teachers. I think he tried to look cheerful.

"Have a seat, please, anywhere you'd like," he said.

So I sat down on his sofa and waited to see what was going to happen. I noticed he had pictures of his wife and kids all over his desk.

"So, Robert, how are you doing today?"

"Fine."

"Well, I'm glad to hear that. Do you like school?"

"Not really."

He sort of laughed.

"Yeah, I remember thinking school was a waste of time when I was your age." Then he said, "Hey, would you like to play a little game with me?"

I thought I probably wouldn't. After all, I'd much rather be outside. But I didn't want to hurt his feelings.

"Sure," I said. I picked at a hangnail on my left pinkie to pass the time.

"Okay, I'm going to say a word and then you say the first word that comes to your mind. Got it?"

"Got it."

"Tree," he said.

"Grass," I said.

"Bone."

"Chicken."

"Truth."

"Lie."

"Red."

"Orange."

"Parents," he said.

Just then I wiggled the hangnail and pulled it off. "Ouch!" I said. It hurt more than I thought it would.

"Well, well," Mr. Wellborn said. For some reason, he looked upset. "That's enough for today. How about if we visit again, maybe toward the end of the week?"

"Sure," I said, and sucked on my sore finger.

"Remember, Robert, I'm here if you want to talk to me before then."

"Thanks," I said and got up. Boy, that was *really* weird, I thought.

Leaving the office, I looked at my watch. Good. It was almost time for lunch. Then art, then reading, and then we would be out of school. Today was the day we started our job.

At three-fifteen, Max and I bolted for our book bags. We had stuffed our kits inside.

The plan was to work about one hour a day. That way we'd make it home by the time soccer practice would have ended. We figured that would be enough time for one or two houses.

We took the bus home from school. We were so excited we nearly missed our stop.

"Whose house do you think we should go to first?" Max asked.

I really hadn't had a chance to think about it. I just said the first name that came into my brain.

"How about Mr. O'Hara?"

"Do you think he'd buy?"

"Yeah, my mom says he's just grumpy because he lives alone and he misses Mrs. O'Hara. But don't say anything to him about us working on Saturday. We're going to be rich. Our horse manure days are over."

"Did you practice the speech?" Max asked. "I memorized it," she said.

"No," I said. "I didn't want to take out my kit last night. My parents were basket cases because I got home so late."

"Yeah, mine too. But since they were so busy yelling at my brother, they were tired out by the time they got to me."

"What'd he do?"

"Well, remember that video camera he got last Christmas?"

"Yeah."

"After school he and Itchy took his camera and filmed the Osckermans next door in secret. They were really boring. Just watching TV and eating, but it looked pretty funny. My parents were really mad."

By then we were almost to Mr. O'Hara's. We sat on the grass and took out our kits to figure out what we were going to say.

"This doesn't make a lot of sense to me," Max said. "Does it to you?"

"Of course it does," I said. "It's only confusing because we've never been in the real business world before. I'll do all the talking. You just smile and take the notes."

"You wish," Max shot back. "This is a fifty-fifty partnership. In fact, I'm thinking of business cards. My uncle Joe is a printer. 'Max Laramax, President,' has a nice ring to it. Vice president for you. I think this is going to your head already, and we haven't seen a dime yet. We could be back in manure tomorrow."

"You win, Max," I said. "We'll take turns talking."

I read over the sheet again and practiced my sales speech.

"Ready?" I asked.

"Affirmative."

"Let's go."

We walked up Mr. O'Hara's long dirt driveway. I didn't expect it, but my heart was pounding so loudly I was afraid Max could hear it. My lips felt as if they were stuck together.

I knocked on the screen door. Mr. O'Hara appeared, wearing this old pair of overalls with holes in the knees.

"Well, I was wondering when you horse thieves were going to show up," he said. "My barn stinks so bad the flies won't even go in."

I forced a smile.

"Actually," I said, "we're here on business."

"Monkey business, no doubt. Well, c'mon in and sit down."

We took a seat at his kitchen table. It was piled high with papers and stuff. But Mr. O'Hara just pushed it all over to the side.

"I'm working on my taxes. You know, now that you kids are businessmen you're going to have to deal with Uncle Sam."

"I don't have an uncle Sam," I said.

Max rolled her eyes and threw me one of her looks.

"Oh you've got one, all right," Mr. O'Hara said, laughing. "That's just another name for the government. So what kind of gizmo are you two trying to sell me today?"

I took out my box of cookies and my sheet with all the questions. I stood up. Since he was my first customer, I had to read just about everything from the sheet.

"I represent Cash-in-Advance Cookies. Now, for just two dollars and ninety-five cents, not only do you get a box of imported cookies, but your name will be entered in our grand-prize drawing. You could win a fabulous prize."

I paused for a minute because my mouth was really dry. Mr. O'Hara got up and brought me a glass of water. "Here you go, son. This is a pretty long spiel you have going."

"Thank you," I said, gulping down the water.

Max jumped in. "Anyway, as you can see, it's an excellent deal."

"Sounds good to me. Sold. I'll take a box," he said.

"Thanks a lot," I said, and read the rest of the sheet that Mr. Louie had given me.

"What would you like to know?" he asked.

"Okay," I said. "The first question is, do you believe in getting away and taking vacations?"

Mr. O'Hara laughed.

"Yes. As often as possible, I try to get down to my brother's horse ranch in Virginia."

"Question number two. Would you be willing to give up all your worldly possessions if it could save a life or help someone else?"

"Yes, I suppose so," he said.

"Well, now that you've answered all the questions, you're eligible to have your name put into our grand-prize drawing."

Max cleared her throat really loud and stepped on my toe under the table. I had forgotten to let her do her part of it.

So Max said, "If you win, we wouldn't want to duplicate any items that you might already have. So I would like to go down a checklist with you and see which prize you would be most interested in. Okay?"

"Okay." He winked at Max.

"Stereo/CD player?"

"Got one."

"Thirty-five millimeter camera?"

"Got one."

"VCR?"

"Got one."

"Microwave?"

"Yep."

"Well, Mr. O'Hara," I said, "it seems like you have a lot of stuff. So our grand prize for you will have to be a surprise."

"Sounds good to me," he said.

"I have one last question," Max said. "If you had to give up your most prized possession to help someone else, which possession would it be?"

"Well, I don't have to think very hard about that one," he said. "I'll show you." He walked over to an old chest he kept locked up.

"You two ought to have fun looking at this."

He unlocked the chest and pulled out a big bag of gold coins. He dumped them on the table. Then he held one up for us to see.

"These gold coins date back to the Civil War. I bought them at an auction almost forty years ago."

"Cool," Max said.

After a few minutes Mr. O'Hara put the coins back in the chest and locked it. "Okay, so now you two know everything there is to know about me. Are you finished?"

"Yes, sir," we said at the same time.

I almost forgot to give him his box of cookies. I handed them over and he gave me three dollars. He told me to keep the change.

We packed up our sales stuff and got ready to go.

"So when do I hear if I win the grand prize?"

"I'm not sure when it is, but we'll let you know."

We were halfway down the dirt driveway when he yelled, "Any chance you executives will be back to help me with the barn?"

"Sure," I yelled. And I kind of meant it. Not that I wanted to shovel horse gook anymore, but I really liked Mr. O'Hara.

"I hope he wins the grand prize," Max said.

"Yeah, me too." She started messing up my hair and said, "So, you do have a heart."

Things were going great. No, even better than great. I never imagined how easy being a salesman was going to be. I mean, Mr. O'Hara bought a box just like that. I figured that at the rate Max and I were going, we'd be rolling in dough by the end of the month.

However, back at school the following day, there was kind of a catch. I was in art class trying to draw what Mrs. Piccatto had asked for — a self-portrait.

Well, I thought it would be funny to make myself look like Freddy Krueger because I knew that would make Max have a laughing fit.

My picture was really good. It looked just like Freddy. I even put some blood on it, dripping down his face and everything. How was I supposed to know they were going to be on display at the Parents' Open House the following week?

At the end of class, we put our drawings into our art folders. But three days later the drawing showed up in front of my face when I had another visit with Mr. Wellborn.

Mr. Wellborn was so nice and so friendly. He really knew how to make a kid feel right at home in his office. He had on another one of those peppy outfits — purple shirt and yellow pants.

When he saw me, the way he treated me you would have thought I was the President of the United States or something.

"Hey, Robert," he said. "You're looking mighty cheerful today." Then he patted the chair where he wanted me to sit. But this time he sat in the chair that was right next to mine, except for a little table in between us.

"How's everything going?" he asked.

"Fine," I said. But I didn't tell him that I was pulling in five thousand dollars a month. He might have been jealous. "Are we going to play some more games today?" I asked.

"Sure," he said, "if that's all right with you."

"Sure. Anything is better than going to chorus."

"Okay, let me get out my family."

The way he said it, I thought he kept Mrs. Wellborn and his kids stuffed inside his desk.

Instead, he took out a bunch of little figures made of plaster or something like that.

They were no bigger than my G.I. Joe figures. There was even a little plaster dog.

"Okay, Robert," he said. "Let's pretend that this is a family. It could be your family, or it could be any family."

"Well, I don't have a sister," I said, pointing to the little girl figure.

"That's okay, it's just pretend."

"Okay."

"Now," he said, "what I want you to do is show me how the people in this family might get along. In other words, pretend that you just got up and you come downstairs, say, and there's the family. Okay?"

"Okay," I said, but I really didn't get it. And I also thought it was really, really weird. But I tried to play along.

Well, the only thing I could think of to do was to pretend those people were a bunch of G.I. Joe's. I wasn't about to act like I was playing with dolls.

So I picked up the two guy figures, one was big and one was small, and I made shooting noises and war cries. I took the big guy and I had him completely cream the little guy.

Meanwhile, Mr. Wellborn took notes like crazy.

Hey, this is kind of fun, I thought. I really got into it. So I had them say things like, "Please, stop. I give up."

Then right in the middle Mr. Wellborn said, "Robert, what about the female figures?"

"Oh, yeah," I said. I figured he wanted them in the fun, too. So I took the biggest guy and I knocked the females over, making my best bomb explosion noise. "Kaboom!"

Well, Mr. Wellborn got the strangest look on his face. All of a sudden he said, "That's enough,

Robert, we're finished playing the game now." He turned his face to me and looked very serious. "Robert," he said, "are you angry at someone?"

"Kind of," I said. Then this started me thinking about two weeks ago when my friend Jeffrey and I were playing G.I. Joe at my house and he knocked me down with a surprise attack. I was covered with mud and I got in a lot of trouble. I must have gotten a mad look on my face just thinking about it because Mr. Wellborn said slowly, "Robert, am I upsetting you to talk about this?"

"Yes," I said.

"Is it because you thought you could trust this person?"

"Exactly," I said. "It just didn't seem fair."

Well, anyway, how was I supposed to know that Mr. Wellborn thought I was talking about my dad when I was really talking about Jeffrey? I mean, my dad is one of the greatest guys in the world and he never even believed in spankings! But I think this is kind of how everything got mixed up.

The next thing Mr. Wellborn said was that he really wanted me to know that he's my friend. I could come and talk to him anytime about anything.

"Anything?" I asked, thinking about my money-making plan. Because if anyone could tell me how to get people to open up to me and answer my questions, he could. So I said, "Well, there is a question I would like to ask you."

"Shoot. Anything," Mr. Wellborn said.

"Well, I'm kind of involved in this new business deal. It's real important to get people to tell me things I need to know."

"Oh, that's very simple, Robert," he said. "People love to talk about themselves. Just ask a question like 'What's your favorite hobby?' Or ask them about something they have displayed in their home. Chances are they're very proud of it and you won't be able to shut them up."

Then he looked at his watch and raised his eyebrows. "I'm afraid we're going to have to stop now. We'll talk again real soon, okay?"

"Okay," I said. I'd do this over music class any day.

By the time I got back to my classroom, it was almost time to go home. I tried to catch Max's eye to see if she'd remembered to bring her sales kit to school, but she was too busy paying attention to the teacher.

I felt like blowing a spitball to get her attention. Then I thought, why not? Mrs. Hunt had her back turned. She wrote our homework assignment on the blackboard.

So I spit in a little piece of paper and rolled it into a hard ball. Then I stuffed the ball inside the straw I kept inside my desk. I was just about to blow it over when Mrs. Hunt screamed, "Robert, don't you dare." That was scary because she never even turned around to see me do it.

No question about it. She really did have eyes in the back of her head.

5.
Mrs. Adamsworth

We had to wait until Thursday to visit our next customer. Max said it looked way too suspicious if we told our parents we had practice every day. But it was really hard to wait another day. Especially now that Mr. Wellborn had given me all those great tips.

During recess on Thursday, most of the kids just played. But Max and I had important things to discuss. We met on a giant rock in back of the jungle gym.

"Max, who do you think we should try to sell next?"

"I was thinking of Mrs. Adamsworth," she said, "that woman who lives on the hill in that awesome mansion."

"Yeah," I agreed, "that's a good idea."

So anyway, we had our plan: Get off the bus. Put on our business outfits. Head for Mrs. Adamsworth's.

When the bell rang at three-fifteen, Mrs. Hunt asked us to turn in our book reports before we left. Well, Max turned in hers, but it had sticky chocolate goop all over one edge.

Mrs. Hunt sniffed the report and went charging for Max's desk. Max tried to stuff three-quarters of a Snickers bar into her mouth, but half of it stuck out. Mrs. Hunt made her go to the bathroom and spit it out.

Since the bell had gone off, I left the classroom and waited out in the hall. But even out there I heard The Iron Lung yelling. That was the first time she yelled at Max.

"How many times do I have to tell you kids there's no eating in my classroom! You, of all people, Margaret Anne. You're supposed to be a leader and set a good example."

Max came out a few minutes later. She was happy I had waited for her.

"That lady is like the Chocolate Police," Max mumbled. Then Max took some M&M's out of her pocket and emptied half the bag into her mouth.

We ran for the bus and barely made it. After we got off at our stop, we had to double back about a mile to get to Mrs. Adamsworth's house. Then I remembered that some kids thought it was haunted.

When we got to her driveway, I kind of slowed down.

"You're not turning chicken on me, are you?" Max asked.

"Nope," I said. "But I've heard that everyone who lives in that house is dead. So how are we going to sell cookies to a dead lady?"

"Robert," she said, "if everyone is dead, then tell me who mows this gigantic lawn?"

That was a good question. It *was* true that no one had ever really seen Mrs. Adamsworth in the last several years, though. I kept walking, figuring that anyone with that kind of money might spring for two boxes. Maybe more.

There were two huge iron gates blocking the front door. We pushed a buzzer on the gate. We waited. And just like in the movies, they opened on their own. We walked through them up to the door. Suddenly I heard dogs barking. I hoped they were chained.

Max took a deep breath. "Don't forget to take really good notes," she said. "I'll do the talking this time." I was just as glad because my teeth chattered like those windup teeth you buy in a joke store.

She slammed the door knocker twice, but nothing happened. I slammed it again even harder. Then the door opened. There she was. Mrs. Adamsworth.

The three of us were looking at each other eyeball to eyeball. She wasn't much bigger than me.

She was kind of skinny like my grandmother. Her voice was low and hoarse.

"Yes?" she asked, slowly.

Max took a few steps forward.

At first when Max tried to speak, nothing came out. She coughed, then tried again.

"Hello, ma'am, I'm Margaret Anne Laramax and this is my friend, Robert. We're here selling Cash-In-Advance Cookies."

"Nice concept," she said. "Come in, my little ones. Don't worry about that barking. Those dogs are locked in their kennel in the back."

The inside was dark. After a few minutes, I could see a little better. She led and we followed. There were so many rooms. They went on and on.

She had this cane that she whacked everything with as she walked. I was glad I wasn't walking in front of her. I could even see little dents in the furniture.

"I'll bet you kids think I'm blind as a bat."

I didn't answer, to be polite. We just followed quietly. I'd never seen a house that big before.

Finally we came to a huge kitchen. There were cabinets everywhere, with rows and rows of dishes.

Mrs. Adamsworth tapped her cane on the kitchen table.

"Take a seat, kids. And no shenanigans. I've still got one good eye. And I raised three children, so don't think you can put anything past me."

Then she walked over to the refrigerator and opened it.

"Well, let's see, we've got liver pâté, no, you wouldn't like that, leftover asparagus with hollandaise, no . . . ah, how about delicious cinnamon raisin bread and some ginger ale."

"Yes, please," I said.

I heard Max's stomach growl. Boy, can that girl eat!

Mrs. Adamsworth cut two slices of bread. Then she poured our ginger ale and put everything on the kitchen table. It took her a long time cause she never put down her cane.

"So, tell me again about this organization . . . Cash-in-Advance Cookies."

I started to talk and got almost halfway through my speech, but Max jumped in and wouldn't stop talking.

I decided she was stealing my show so I interrupted. "Yes, and if you buy their cookies, you could be a grand-prize winner."

Mrs. Adamsworth got a weird look.

I tried to continue but Max beat me to it. "Yes, if you buy our cookies, you're eligible to enter our grand-prize drawing. If your name is selected, the prize is picked especially for you."

"Is that right?" she asked. "Well, go ahead, dear, this is very interesting."

Then I got out my list of questions. I went through them in my own style.

First I asked her, "Do you have a VCR?"

"No."

"Camera?"

"Yes."

"TV?"

"Yes."

And on and on until we got to the end.

Then I started my personal questions. First I asked: "What is your most prized possession?"

"Oh, my," she said, "I have so many I don't know where to begin."

Here's where I kept real quiet, like Mr. Wellborn taught me. It worked like a charm.

"This house is full of wonderful things. C'mon, I'll give you kids the grand tour."

Once again, she picked up her cane and we followed. Max took the rest of her bread with her.

She led us through three long hallways and up a gigantic winding staircase. Portraits lined the walls. She pointed to them with her cane.

"These portraits are three generations of Adamsworths. My great-great-great grandfather came over on the *Mayflower*."

"Wow," Max and I said at the same time.

Every portrait had an interesting story behind it. It was like getting a real-life history lesson.

Finally, we all walked back down to the kitchen and sat at the table.

"So," she said, "let me see these cookies. How much are they? Two ninety-five? When I was little, cookies cost five cents for a box. And stamps were two cents. I used to walk three miles to school. My parents were very poor."

"Wow," I said, thinking she had come a long way to live in a house like this.

"Well, the thing I remember most," she said, "is my folks never lost their spirit or their sense of humor."

The clock in the hallway chimed really loud. I looked at my watch. It was five o'clock.

"We've got to get going," I said, and jumped up. I hoped I wasn't rude.

"Well, here, let me take a box of cookies. Make that two." Then she opened a drawer and pulled out six brand-new dollar bills. I gave her back a dime.

We collected our stuff and followed her to the front door.

"This has been one of the most pleasant afternoons I've had in a long, long time, kids. Will you visit again?" she asked.

"Sure," Max promised. "I would love to hear more about your great-great-great-grandfather's trip on the *Mayflower*."

"Me, too," I said.

"If you two come by after school next Tuesday, I'll hunt for some of my old Indian relics to show you."

"Great," we both said at once and waved good-bye.

I felt so good I almost hugged Max. Our first

week on the job. Every customer was a sale. And five thousand dollars in the mail!

I couldn't wait to see my dad's face when I showed him all that money. Maybe I'd even give him some of it.

6.
The Big Sales Meeting

I could hardly wait for Monday to arrive. I knew Mr. Louie and Mr. Lloyd would be impressed when they saw how well we had done.

When the school bell rang at three-fifteen, Max and I did our usual routine. We stood out in the parking lot and waited for Vinnie.

"Hey, Max," I said, "what do you think Mr. Louie and Mr. Lloyd are going to say when we tell them we have two customers?"

"They'll probably give us a raise or something," she said. *Boom! Kur-put!* The sound nearly blew out our ear drums. "I guess Vinnie must be close by," Max said, smirking.

Within seconds, there he was with that stupid grin shouting, "What's shakin'?"

"Hi, Vinnie," I said.

"Yeah, hi," Max grunted.

"Same place, same station?" he asked.

"Yes," we replied.

51

"Well, you guys are running up quite a bill with my taxi service. Today I expect to get paid."

"Look," I said, "if you pick us up at about four-thirty, we'll be able to pay you. We're getting paid today."

"Oooh," Vinnie said, his mouth round. "You guys are big time. Hey, maybe they'll hire me."

Not a chance, I thought. Then Max said, "Well, we're not hiring right now, but I'll let you know if there are any openings." Vinnie gave her a dirty look in the rearview mirror.

This time when we got to 423 King Street we weren't as nervous. We were big time now.

Vinnie pulled up to the curb and we jumped out.

"Four-thirty sharp," Max shouted to the car.

"Oh, I'll be here, all right," Vinnie yelled back. "Remember, it's payday."

We walked up the two flights of steps. I knocked on the door, and it opened just a little, like last time. I could see Mr. Louie's nose poking through the space.

"You guys are right on time," he said. "What's the password?"

I gulped. I didn't remember anything about a password.

"Just kidding," Mr. Louie said with his big, roaring laugh. The door opened wide and we went inside.

"Please excuse the mess," he said. "The cleaning lady just isn't doing her job."

"Oh, we don't mind," I said. "Looks kind of like my room."

Mr. Louie walked over to the couch and shook Mr. Lloyd really hard. He was snoring.

"Mr. Lloyd," he said. "Our top salespeople are here." Mr. Lloyd woke up and we started our meeting. Max and I sat down on the couch. Mr. Louie and Mr. Lloyd pulled up a couple of chairs.

"Well, guys, are you ready to talk business?"

We nodded.

"Take a look at these sales figures," I said, taking out our sheets with the names of our customers and the amount they paid.

Mr. Louie was so excited he grabbed them. Then he read out loud.

"Mr. O'Hara: two dollars and ninety-five cents. Mrs. Adamsworth: five dollars and ninety cents (might buy more)."

"Max, Robert," he said, leaning his face in real close, "these are impressive numbers, very impressive. Don't you think so, Mr. Lloyd?"

Mr. Lloyd looked really happy. He nodded.

"You didn't forget to ask those very important questions, did you?"

I proudly pulled out the two sheets.

The sheets almost got torn in half because Mr. Louie and Mr. Lloyd tried to pull them out of my hands at the same time. Then they nearly bumped heads trying to read the answers to the questions we had asked Mr. O'Hara.

Mr. Louie looked especially excited. "Is this Mr. O'Hara guy rich?" he asked.

"Yes," Max said. "He collects antiques. He told us he buys them at auctions."

"Oh, yeah," I chimed in. "He even had this big bag of gold coins."

"They're from the Civil War," Max added.

Well, you should have seen their faces. They lit up like pinball machines on a triple play.

"Gold coins, did you say?" Mr. Lloyd asked.

"Yes. But he keeps them all locked up in a secret chest."

Then Mr. Louie and Mr. Lloyd read out loud the list of items Mr. O'Hara had in his home. "VCR, microwave . . ."

Mr. Louie and Mr. Lloyd laughed hard, but I didn't get what was so funny. They laughed so hard that they held their bellies and tears were running down their faces.

When they finally stopped, Mr. Louie said, "Sorry, kid, don't take it personal or nothin'."

"So," Mr. Lloyd said, "let's see the other customer's sheet." I handed him the notes we took at Mrs. Adamsworth's house.

"You both did an excellent job," Mr. Louie said. "Now, did you get any juicy details about Mrs. Adamsworth?"

"Boy, did we ever," I said. "I used my special questioning sales technique."

"And what exactly did you find out?" Mr. Lloyd asked.

"Well," I said, "she had relatives that came over on the *Mayflower.*"

"Yes," Max added, "real Pilgrims."

"And she has these huge portraits of them all over."

"Sounds like a very nice house," Mr. Louie said.

"House! It's a mansion! You should see this place. It even has statues," I said.

"Oh, we'll make it a point to visit this lady. It sounds like she could get very lonely in that big place, doesn't it, Mr. Louie?"

"Oh, yeah. Maybe we could pick up a pizza and pay her a little visit. Does she live with anyone?" Mr. Louie asked.

"Well," I said, "her husband died not too long ago. She usually has a butler, and a gardener, too. But they're off this week, so she was kind of lonely."

"Well, I have the feeling she might even get a visit from The Cookie Kings themselves, up close and personal."

"Maybe she could be next week's grand-prize winner," I suggested.

"Well, Scouts, it's time to turn over your earnings."

I reached inside my book bag and pulled out the money. Mr. Louie counted it.

55

"Two ninety-five plus five ninety, that's about nine dollars according to my calculations."

I nodded.

"Good work, guys. Put out your hands," Mr. Louie said. "Here's a dollar for you, Robert. And here's a dollar for you, Max."

Max and I just looked at each other. It wasn't even enough to pay Vinnie for the ride. Not to mention the other money we owed him.

"What about the five thousand dollars?" Max asked. "When do we get that?"

Mr. Lloyd and Mr. Louie exchanged smiles. "You know, those are the kind of questions that make us know you were the right two for this job."

I breathed relief.

"The five thousand dollars, as we explained before, comes from the prize pool."

"So we're not going to get paid right away?" Max asked.

"Exactly," Mr. Louie said.

"Well, should we just keep on with our sales work?" I asked.

"Oh, yes, by all means."

"You see," Mr. Louie added, "it takes us a few days to figure out your commissions — you know where I'm comin' from?"

Max could have probably calculated it on the spot, but I said, "Oh, I get it. You'll send us a check in the mail or something."

"Exactly!" Mr. Louie said again.

I looked at my watch. It was four-thirty-five. We were supposed to meet Vinnie outside at four-thirty. I knew he'd be mad since Max told him not to be late. But he'd be foaming at the mouth when he heard we didn't have his money.

Max and I picked up our stuff and said good-bye.

"Same time next week?" I asked.

"Count on it," Mr. Louie said. "Oh, by the way, do you kids still take care of that fancy parrot?"

"Yes," I said. "I even taught it to burp."

"Oh, now that's talent," Mr. Louie said, laughing.

When we got downstairs, Vinnie was there. He revved up his engine like a lunatic.

"He's such a show-off," Max whispered.

We opened the rusty car door and climbed in.

"Hi, Vinnie," I said real friendly.

"Hey, squirts. So what kind of big business deals are you two pulling off?"

"Well," I said, "we can't talk about it right now."

"That's okay. I'm only interested in the green stuff. You guys owe me two bucks from Monday, six bucks for today, and a buck for interest."

"That's highway robbery," Max growled. "If you'll pardon the pun."

Vinnie just laughed, stuck one hand out, and steered with the other.

I was kind of afraid to tell him we only had two bucks. You never knew with Vinnie. He might have kicked us out right in the middle of nowhere.

Then, luckily, I got this idea. "Hey, Vinnie, if you let us pay you next week, we'll pay you even more interest."

"No, what you mean is you'll pay me double the entire amount."

"No, but we'll make it an even twenty-five dollars," Max said. Maybe she figured we'd get our huge check in the mail within three or four days.

Vinnie conceded, "Okay, okay."

He dropped Max off first, then me.

I walked in the door and smelled bread baking.

"Is that you, Robert?" my mom called.

"The one and only."

I ran up the steps to my bedroom and shoved the book bag under my bed. Then I went back down into the kitchen.

"Hi, guy. How was practice?" she asked.

"Great," I replied.

"By the way, Robert, I got a very strange call today."

"Oh, yeah?"

"It was from a Mrs. Walker. She said she was a counselor from the school district."

I had been munching on a cookie. This stopped me dead in the middle of it.

"Yes, and she said she wanted to come pay us a visit."

My mom wiped her hands on her apron.

"Did she say why?" I asked and nearly choked on my cookie.

"No, that was the strange part. She didn't even say exactly when she was coming. She just said she would 'drop in' soon."

"Robbie, are you in some kind of trouble?" she asked. Her face looked so sweet and worried.

I shrugged. "Not that I know of," I replied.

Now I wasn't exactly lying. Because, believe me, I had no idea how much trouble I was in.

7.
The Robbery

My dad always said to never make a promise you don't plan to keep. And since I promised Mrs. Adamsworth that Max and I would show up on Tuesday, we did.

Max and I got off the bus at our usual stop and walked the mile back to Mrs. Adamsworth's house. Only this time we were really looking forward to it. Even her driveway looked friendly that day.

When we knocked on the door, she seemed surprised. I don't think she thought we'd really show up.

"Why, Max, Robert, come on in." She kind of pointed the way with her cane.

Again, we walked through a million gigantic rooms till we got to the kitchen.

"Have a seat. I called in an order to Sweeney's and had it delivered."

Sweeney's was my mom's favorite bakery. Mrs.

Adamworth gave each of us a chocolate eclair and a glass of milk.

"Did you find all of your old Indian stuff?" I asked.

"I said I would, didn't I?" she said. Then she gave me a wink and left the room.

Max had already wolfed down the entire eclair before Mrs. Adamsworth came back. When she returned, she was holding an old key in her hand.

"When you kids are finished, I'm going to show you a real sight," she said, smiling.

I stuffed the rest in my mouth and finished my milk. Then Max and I stood up.

"Ready," I said.

This time we went through the back of the kitchen and wound around through a few more rooms. We finally came to a locked door. Mrs. Adamsworth put the key in the keyhole, and the door opened. She flipped on a light and we followed her up the long narrow staircase.

When we got to the top, she flipped on another light. I've never seen an attic so filled with stuff in my life. It was totally awesome.

"Careful, darlings. There's lots to trip over," she said.

Max and I followed her over to a large trunk. It was sitting in front of a great big wardrobe.

The trunk was really old. I helped Mrs. Adamsworth pry the top open. And wow! Inside it looked like something you'd see in a museum.

There was a real tomahawk, a pair of Indian moccasins, and a real bow and arrow.

Max pulled out the Indian headdress.

"Put it on," Mrs. Adamsworth said.

Max put it on her head. Then I pulled out a tomahawk and this Indian drum. We both pretended to do a war dance. I waved the tomahawk and Max pounded the drum.

Mrs. Adamsworth even gave out a war cry. We were all having so much fun. But when we finally stopped laughing, we heard voices downstairs.

"Sh, sh, sh," Mrs. Adamsworth said suddenly. Then she whispered, "Someone's in the house!"

I thought my heart was going to jump through my chest.

Mrs. Adamsworth picked up her cane and very slowly crept over to the top of the staircase.

We all heard a crash. "Robbers," Mrs. Adamsworth whispered to us. "Stay very still."

We heard voices, so we knew there must be at least two of them.

Then one robber screamed that he found the silver. The other yelled, "Help me get the paintings down!"

We all huddled together and held hands, listening.

"We could have used a truck to take away this haul. Check out these statues."

Max and I instantly looked at each other. We knew those voices! The big job was just a big joke. All my plans for the money disappeared.

Then we heard the robber talking about taking "the picture of the old dude" hanging over the fireplace. That was their big mistake. Because suddenly Mrs. Adamsworth seemed about fifty years younger and a hundred times stronger.

"Over my dead body they'll take that picture," she said loudly.

Before we could stop her, she was on her way down the stairs.

Max and I didn't move. Then we heard a lot of screaming and yelling.

"Come on," Max said. "We can't leave her down there alone. This whole thing *is* kind of our fault. In a way."

Suddenly, we heard a loud crash and Mrs. Adamsworth screamed, "Let me go."

That did it. We went flying through the attic and down the stairs to the living room.

Mr. Louie and Mr. Lloyd were wearing women's stockings over their heads. They looked silly. They even had on rubber gloves like my mom wears when she washes the dishes. I guess they didn't want to leave any fingerprints. But their bellies hung out over their pants, so I knew it was them right away.

Mr. Louie held the portrait in his hands, and Mrs. Adamsworth whacked him every which way with her cane. "Give me back that portrait, you two-bit crook," she yelled.

Then Mr. Louie yelled to Mr. Lloyd, who was dragging one of the statues toward the door, "Lloyd, get her off of me."

At first, Max and I just stood there, watching the action. Nobody noticed us.

Then Mr. Lloyd put down the statue and pulled Mrs. Adamsworth's cane from her hands, and I finally snapped out of it.

"Let her go," I screamed, running to help.

Mr. Louie and Mr. Lloyd looked totally shocked to see me and Max.

"Do what he says," Max screamed. I was glad to have her support.

"Well, if it ain't Bonnie and Clyde," Mr. Lloyd said under his breath. Then he glared at us and whispered, "One word to the cops and you're going to jail with us. You two signed a contract, remember? That makes you accessories to a crime!"

I was frozen with fear. Max ran for the phone, but Mr. Louie stopped her. Mrs. Adamsworth was still whacking him over the head.

"Louie, tie 'em up. Get the lady first before I don't have a brain left."

"You'll do no such thing!" Mrs. Adamsworth screamed, and I caught her eye. She mouthed the words "the dogs, the dogs" and jerked her head in the direction of the kennel. Mr. Louie and Mr.

Lloyd were so busy tying up Mrs. Adamsworth that they didn't see me run outside.

I went over to the kennel gate and undid the latch. Two giant black Dobermans leaped out of the kennel and raced toward the house, barking like crazy!

I ran back inside after them. By the time I got to the living room the bigger dog had sunk his teeth into Mr. Louie's butt.

Mr. Lloyd was fending off the other dog with the fireplace poker.

"Call off your dogs!" Mr. Louie yelled. "Then nobody will get hurt."

Mrs. Adamsworth didn't trust them one bit.

"If you two hoodlums aren't out of here in two seconds, I'll let them rip you to bits! Zeus, Athena, stay," she commanded. The dogs obeyed but continued to growl.

Mr. Louie and Mr. Lloyd dropped everything and ran for the door. We heard them speed off.

"Are you kids all right?" Mrs. Adamsworth asked.

"Yeah, I think so," I said. I looked over at Max, "Are you okay, Max?" She just nodded her head.

"Well," Mrs. Adamsworth said, "this is more excitement than I was counting on for a Tuesday afternoon."

"We've never seen those men before in our lives," I said a little too loudly.

"Well, I'm sure you haven't," she agreed. "Those two-bit crooks are only fit to associate with the rats."

"Lower than rats," I added. All this for a stupid Super Soaker, I'm thinking.

"Well, we need to call the police," Mrs. Adamsworth said. "Can you take care of it for me?"

I called 911. When I was telling Max and Mrs. Adamsworth that the police were on their way, I heard a siren before I even finished my sentence. Two police officers came in.

"Is anyone hurt in here? Do you need an ambulance?" one of the police officers said.

"No," Mrs. Adamsworth said, "we're just a bit shaken up."

The female officer took out a report form and pen.

"I'm Officer Curry," she said. "This is my partner, Officer Hernandez."

She took down our names and addresses. Then she asked, "Can you tell me what happened? Was there more than one?"

I held my breath, wishing I was invisible.

"There were two of them," Mrs. Adamsworth said. "They didn't take anything, as far as I know. We set the dogs on them and they ran like the dickens."

The police officers mostly talked to Mrs. Adamsworth.

"Any chance it could have been anyone you

know — anyone familiar with the layout of the house?"

Mrs. Adamsworth shook her head. "I've never seen the likes of those two anywhere. But if I ever see them again, they'll curse the day they met me. I'll tell you that!"

"Were you able to get a good look at them?" Officer Hernandez asked.

"Both short and fat," Mrs. Adamsworth said confidently. "Maybe fortyish. They were wearing stockings over their heads, but I could see that the taller one had two gold front teeth. Terrible grammar. Oh, and they wore those rubber gloves that one might wear when doing dishes."

The cop looked at me, then Max. "Do either of you have anything to add?"

I shook my head. I was afraid that if I talked they would know by my voice that I was lying. Max just stayed quiet.

Mrs. Adamsworth hugged Max. "Let's leave these poor children out of it," she said. "Nothing was actually taken, and they're upset enough as it is."

I nodded for emphasis.

"I'm leaving on holiday tomorrow," Mrs. Adamsworth added, "but I'll be glad to come down to the station now and look through some pictures, if you wish."

"That would be great, ma'am," Officer Curry said. "Can I offer you kids a lift home?"

"No thanks," I said. "I think we'd like to walk. It's only a few blocks."

"Okay." The officer handed me and Max a card. "Call me if you remember anything that might be important."

I stuck the card in my pocket. Mrs. Adamsworth walked Max and me to the door.

"I'll be back from London at the end of the month," she said. "I'm going to make it my business to find some relics to bring back for my two favorite heroes."

"That would be great," I said. I tried to smile but it wouldn't happen. My lips were shaking.

"Thanks again, kids," she said and gave us each a kiss on the forehead. "If it weren't for the two of you, I might not have been so lucky."

I don't know why, but I shook my head in agreement.

Max and I didn't say much on the way home. We were totally out of it. Max asked me if I thought we would go to jail.

"I don't know," I said. "I wonder what was on that contract we signed anyway? I just hope no one finds out the truth."

"I wish we'd never seen their ugly faces," Max said.

That night I crawled into my bed at seven-thirty. I fell right to sleep. I dreamed I went to prison. Max was my cellmate. It was horrible. The guard sounded like Pogo and kept telling us to shut up. Then he'd get real nice and say, "You look marvelous!"

The worst part of the whole dream was that Vinnie was our only visitor.

8.
Lousy Lloyd
and Lucky Louisano

The next morning I overslept. My mom had to wake me. She was shaking me back and forth like I was some kind of rolling pin.

"Robbie, wake up. We all overslept." Then she felt my head.

"Do you feel okay, Rob? You hardly ate any dinner last night. And you went to bed without me having to even tell you."

My eyes popped open. I was so happy to see my mom I hugged her.

"Gee," she said smiling, "what did I do to deserve that?"

"Nothing," I said. "I just felt like it."

"Well, I'm going to run downstairs and stick in a piece of toast for you."

"Pop Tarts," I said.

"Okay, Pop Tarts — just hurry. I'm going to have to drive you to school again or you'll be late."

I was up and dressed in no time. I brushed my teeth and went downstairs for breakfast. My dad

70

had already left. My mom was sitting at the table reading the newspaper.

"How about that," she said out loud.

"What?" I asked.

"There's a front-page story about two robberies. Right here in our neighborhood. A Mrs. Adamsworth and, oh, my gosh, Mr. O'Hara next door."

My heart flew into overdrive. I couldn't believe it. Mr. O'Hara, too! I almost started to cry. I held my breath, afraid of what would happen next.

"Wow," she continued. "She was able to identify them. It says they're pretty sure it was two con men. They're known as Lousy Lloyd and Lucky Louisano."

"Lucky?"

"Let's see, it says they got their names from a warden at the San Quentin Penitentiary, where they escaped from four months ago. Lousy Lloyd was known for his ruthless behavior toward other inmates. And Lucky Louisano was able to pull off a number of con jobs without being apprehended. Oh, the police suspect they have left the area and are on their way to Mexico. Look at this — they've even put a ten-thousand-dollar reward on their heads."

I tried to chew my Pop Tart, but it felt stuck in my throat.

My mom checked her watch and threw down the paper. "We have to go this minute or I'll have to write you another late excuse," she said.

I jumped up. My mom handed me my lunch and drove me to school.

I zipped into the classroom just before the bell went off. Max was already in her seat.

Mrs. Hunt was writing assignments on the blackboard.

I leaned over my desk and tried to get Max's attention.

"Psst. Psst. Max," I whispered.

"No talking," Mrs. Hunt commanded without turning around.

I waited another minute. "Psst. Max. Turn around." Max's ears must have been clogged.

"*Excuse* me," Mrs. Hunt said.

"Why, did you burp or something?" the kid behind me asked.

Everybody laughed. That was until Mrs. Hunt turned around and I saw her face. She was actually snarling and showing her teeth.

"Who said that?" she demanded. The class was dead quiet.

"All right, if no one wants to own up to it, then the whole class will pay. No recess today. You will all remain inside quietly at your desks. You have your very rude classmate to thank for this."

I was dying to talk to Max about the newspaper and everything. Maybe we could try and talk at lunch, I thought. I just didn't want anyone to hear us.

Right before lunch, Mrs. Hunt called me up to her desk.

"Yes?" I asked.

"Mr. Wellborn had to cancel your appointment today. He said he'll make another one next week. How are things going at home, Robert? Any better?"

What was she talking about? I thought.

"Somewhat better," I replied.

I had forgotten all about Mr. Wellborn and everything. I wished everybody else would forget, too.

At lunchtime I saved Max a seat. "Max, over here," I yelled. She hurried over and sat beside me.

"Did you see the newspaper?" I whispered in her ear.

"Yeah. That's all my parents talked about this morning. They're afraid our house could be hit next."

"Max, you heard what Mr. Louie said on his way out. If we squeal, we're dead. I wish we hadn't signed anything. I wish we'd never seen their stupid faces. Well, I just hope they get caught," I said.

"Robert," she said as she looked inside my ear. "Sometimes I wonder if they removed your brain last year instead of your tonsils!"

"What do you mean?" I asked.

"What I mean is if Mr. Louie and Mr. Lloyd get caught, *we* get caught."

"Oh, yeah," I said.

"I just keep wondering how we could have been so stupid," I said.

"Maybe we should have asked them to tell us more about themselves. Or maybe we should have told our parents what we were doing," Max said.

"Well," I said, "it's too late for any of that now. I'm scared. Every time the phone rang last night I thought it was the police coming for me. I can't stand this much longer."

"Well, we should have known no one was going to pay us five thousand dollars a month for just selling cookies," Max said. "We shouldn't have fallen for it."

"Yeah. I don't care if we have to sit for a million pets. I'd rather make money that way."

The bell rang. Lunch was over. But the horror continued.

The next couple of days were pretty awful. I just kept wondering when those crooks would be caught. Then I would get scared thinking that they would turn us in, too.

However, by the third day, both of us started to relax a little. Nothing bad had happened yet. Maybe we really were off the hook. I figured Mr. Louie and Mr. Lloyd were probably in Mexico by now.

The rest of the week seemed normal. Max and I even passed out fliers all over the neighborhood to expand our pet-sitting business. We decided to include pet shampoos and obedience school. We decided to add Zeus and Athena to our client base, so we could pay Vinnie back faster. We even got three new calls.

Life was looking pretty good again.

9.
The Letter

By Saturday morning, I couldn't wait to get started on our visits to the new customers. I was about to phone Max when I heard my dad yell from downstairs.

"Rob, you got mail today. I'll leave it on the kitchen table. I'll be back in about an hour. I'm going to get my hair cut."

"Thanks, Dad," I called back. I love to get mail. I figured it was probably something I sent away for with my cereal box tops, so I flew down the steps to get it. The outside of the envelope looked a little weird. My last name and street name were spelled wrong, and the envelope was sealed with lots of tape.

I had to use my teeth to tear it open. When I pulled out the letter, it looked like something out of a movie. It was a piece of paper with all different-size words from magazines. The words were glued all over the page. It read:

HAND OVER THE PARROT OR
ELSE. BRING IT IN A BROWN BOX.
DROP AT 6TH AND SAMSON TODAY.
3PM. IF YOU GO TO COPS YOU WILL
WISH YOU WAS NEVER BORN.

My heart pounded like wild. I thought those crooks were gone for good, but now it looked like Max and I were goners. I took the letter and ran upstairs to call Max.

"Hello," Mrs. Laramax answered.

"Hi, Mrs. Laramax," I said trying to keep my voice from shaking. "Is Max there?"

"Yes, she is. Who's calling please?"

"This is Robert Lawrence."

"Robert?" she asked. "It doesn't sound like you."

"Oh, that's because I'm eating an apple," I said.

"I see. I wish I could get Max to eat fruit," she said. "I'll put her on."

"Hello," Max finally said.

"Max, you're just not going to believe this. Is your mom still standing right there?"

"No. She just went upstairs."

"Okay, listen. Don't panic, but I got this letter in the mail today. It's from Mr. Louie and Mr. Lloyd. We're being blackmailed!"

"Oh, Robert, what are we going to do now?" she whispered.

"Max, they're saying that if we don't give Pogo

to them by three o'clock today they're going to do something horrible."

"See what I mean about telling stories, Robert?" she snapped. "Why did you make up that story about Pogo being so valuable anyway?"

"How could I have known this stuff was going to happen? Look, we need to figure something out. We're in this together, Max. Remember?"

Max was silent for a moment.

Then she yelled, "We could wind up in jail. We signed our names on that contract! They'll blame us for that robbery, too."

By this point I was a screaming lunatic.

"We both have to calm down," Max said. "We need to keep clear heads."

"Max," I said very calmly, "if they know where *I* live, then they also know where *you* live. We have to come up with something."

"Like what?"

"I don't know. We don't have any choice. Somehow we have to think of a way to give them what they want. Meet me over at Mrs. Rice's in exactly one hour. Maybe while we're feeding the bird we'll think of something."

"Okay," Max said. Then we both hung up.

I stuffed the blackmail letter inside my jeans pocket. Then I brushed my teeth. I felt like someone might be watching me. I was even afraid to go to the bathroom.

I went into my room and sat on the bed. I couldn't believe Mr. Louie and Mr. Lloyd would do this to us. They were lower than low.

Then I heard my mom in the hallway.

I pretended like I was reading a comic book.

"Hey, Rob. I just wanted to tell you that Mrs. Carson called this morning while you were still sleeping. She said to keep Sugar away from those sticker bushes when you walk her today. She left the key under the mat."

"Okay. Thanks, Mom," I said, but the last thing I wanted to do was walk that dumb poodle. If Mrs. Carson didn't put all those bows in Sugar's hair, it wouldn't get caught in everything.

I looked at my watch. Ten-thirty. It was time to go meet Max. I finished getting dressed, then I said good-bye to my mom and headed for Mrs. Rice's.

Oddly enough, I had to wait for Max. Normally, she was Miss Punctuality. I started to worry.

Finally, she showed up wearing her mom's giant sunglasses. She looked like a fly.

"Max," I said. "Do you think they're not going to recognize you because you have those glasses on?"

I tried to yank them off but she blocked my hand.

"Let me see the letter," Max said.

I looked around before I took it out of my

pocket. Then I handed it to Max. Her sunglasses fell off while she was reading it. Her eyes were as big as two hamburgers.

"What do you think they'll do to us if we don't give them the bird?" she gulped. Max pointed to the words "OR ELSE." "What do you think that means?" she asked.

"Just what it says. I don't know," I said, feeling jittery.

I folded the letter up and put it back in my pocket. Then we went inside to feed Pogo.

Max and I walked into the kitchen. Pogo was asleep, perched on the bar in his cage. The minute he saw us he started yakking, "Shut up! Shut up!"

Then he started his "You look marvelous" routine. It was enough to make me crazy.

Max brought over the box of food Mrs. Rice left on the counter. I took out Pogo's water bottle and filled it.

I just looked at Pogo and wondered what Mrs. Rice would say if she came home and found him missing. It was kind of hard to think because the bird was squawking like crazy.

After I fed Pogo, I stuck my finger inside the cage and he climbed on. Then I took him out and rubbed his old beak with the special oil. Max refused to do this part because Pogo tried to bite her once. I don't think Pogo really liked Max.

Every time I looked into Pogo's little parrot

eyes I wondered what those creeps planned to do with him. All of a sudden I got a brilliant idea.

"Hey, Max," I said. "What if we don't deliver Pogo?"

"Are you crazy? Do you want to go to jail?"

"No, Max, what I mean is, what if we buy a different bird and put it in the box?"

"That won't work," Max said. "They know Pogo talks."

"Yeah," I agreed, "but what if we put a note in with the new bird and say that the bird only talks to people he really knows."

"Great idea, Rob! They probably won't even talk to the bird until they're long gone."

Then Max's face got sour again.

"Wait a minute, where are we going to get another parrot?"

"Max," I said. "Do you really think those guys know the difference between a parrot and a parakeet? Pogo probably has a higher IQ than they do. They'll just think the bird is too scared to talk."

"Well," she asked. "where are we going to get a parakeet?"

"Where else? We'll go to the pet store at the mall."

I put out my hand and slapped Max a high five. Max put up her hand reluctantly. Then I put Pogo back in his cage. I locked the front door and put the key back under the mat.

We still had to go over to Mrs. Carson's house and walk Sugar. We ran to save time, but when we got to Mrs. Carson's house, Sugar had already done her doggy business on the kitchen floor.

"Max," I said, "why don't you clean it up and I'll walk Sugar."

"No way," Max said. "You clean it and I'll walk Sugar."

Then I saw the note on the counter. It read:

Dear Robert and/or Max:

Please give Sugar a good brushing, but be careful not to ruin the bows I had put on her at the beauty parlor. Also please don't let her wee-wee on my gardenia bushes. Thank you.

Mrs. C.

"All right," I said. "You take the stupid dog outside. I'll clean the floor. Otherwise we'll never get out of here."

I grabbed the paper towels and started cleaning up fast. We had to get a new parakeet in the next two hours and drop it off by 3:00 P.M. Or else.

Max finally came back in with Sugar.

"Okay," I said, thinking out loud. "Now how are we going to get to the mall?"

"Vinnie?" Max groaned.

"But we already owe him so much money. You know he'll charge us some crazy amount."

"Who else could we call?" Max asked.

I knew we were stuck. Time was running out.

"Vinnie's it," I said. "I'll call him."

I used Mrs. Carson's phone and dialed Vinnie's number. Vinnie answered the phone. I could tell he was going to give me a hard time. At this point I would have agreed to anything. He said it would cost us fifteen dollars plus three car washes and waxes.

I hung up the phone.

"Okay, Vinnie's going to pick us up here. He said to wait out front, and that he's only doing this out of the kindness of his heart."

"Yeah, right," Max said. "He gets ten bucks tops. And no car washes. I'll handle him. Is he coming over now?"

I shrugged. "He said he'll get here when he gets here."

Meanwhile, Sugar escaped to the upstairs. I had to take off my sock to try to coax her out from under Mrs. Carson's bed.

When I finally got the sock out of her mouth, it was soaked with dog drool. I just stuffed it in my pocket.

I locked the door and we waited outside. Vinnie pulled up after about a half an hour. This time he had a girl with him.

"Hi, squirts. Hop in."

Max and I climbed in the backseat. It was filled with trash, as usual.

Then Vinnie revved the engine and we jerked

away, leaving a trail of dust. I guess he was trying to impress his girlfriend.

"Carla, these are the two I was telling you about. Guys, this is Carla."

Carla turned around and looked at us. I couldn't believe that a girl that beautiful would go out with Vinnie. She had the blondest hair I'd ever seen. And these beautiful long red nails. She looked like a movie star.

"They're so cute," she said to Vinnie. Then she winked at me.

I felt my cheeks get hot.

It took us about ten minutes to get to the mall. Carla and Vinnie decided to wait in the car while Max and I went inside to buy the parakeet.

When we got out of the car, Carla handed me two dollars and asked me if I would get her some nail polish remover from the drugstore. I felt my face get real red.

"Sure," I said, not even looking at her.

"Robert, we've got to hurry," Max said. "She can do her own shopping."

"I know. I know."

There must have been about one hundred parakeets to choose from. Max decided on the biggest one. She said it would look more like a parrot. It cost four dollars and fifty cents. Since we didn't have any money to buy a cage, the lady gave us a box with holes in it.

I paid for the bird, then we ran to the drugstore.

"Just pick a bottle," Max screamed. She grabbed some nail polish remover from the shelf. We paid for it and raced to the car.

I handed Carla her nail polish remover and change. Then she blew me a kiss. My face was probably the color of tomato soup. It sure felt hot.

"Where to, comrades?" Vinnie asked. "The meter's running."

"Just drop us at the corner of Fifth and Samson," Max said. "And wait for us. We'll be back in a few minutes."

"Is this part of your pet-sitting business?" Vinnie asked, a little suspiciously.

"Yes," I said, thinking fast. "We now do pet deliveries."

"I hope for your sake it pays well," Vinnie added.

I was too nervous to answer him. I checked my watch. We had just ten minutes to get there. I felt sick to my stomach. I handed Max the box so I could roll down the window. I needed some air.

Max poked her nose into the box. She must have said "shut up" a hundred times to that bird.

"Max," I said, "how many times do I have to tell you. You can't train a parakeet to talk. Only parrots talk."

"Well," Max said, "it couldn't hurt to try." Then she whispered, "What do you think they'll do to us if they find out this isn't Pogo?"

"Let's just hope they are far, far away before they do," I whispered back.

Then I took a piece of paper out of my pocket and wrote:

Pogo won't talk if he's scared.

I stuck the note inside the box, and before I knew it we were there.

"You can stop right here," I said to Vinnie.

"I'll wait here for you," Max said. "If that's okay with you."

"You mean you're not coming with me?" I asked.

There was no time to argue with her. I got out of the car holding onto the box and ran one block until I reached Sixth and Samson. Then I placed the box on the sidewalk by the No Parking sign. I felt drops of sweat on my upper lip. I was terrified they would jump out and grab me. I ran back to the car, locked the door as soon as I got in, and scrunched down in the seat.

Vinnie turned around and stared at me.

"Well, where's my dough? They must have paid you when you dropped off the bird."

"You're not going to believe this," I said. "No one was even home. I had to leave the box on the front steps. They'll send the money in the mail."

Vinnie was mad. "You guys are pushing your luck with me," he warned.

Then we took off again, with the wheels spinning. Carla laughed and gave him a kiss on the cheek.

"You'll get your money," I said. I was so relieved it was over. I could tell Max was, too.

We were both quiet on the way home. Vinnie dropped us off in front of Mrs. Rice's house. That way our parents wouldn't see us.

When I got out of the car, my legs felt really weak. Max said hers were, too. We put our arms around each other's shoulders for support.

"Feel like coming over to my house?" I asked.

"Nah," she said. "I just want to go home."

"Yeah. I know what you mean. I'm so glad we're rid of those crooks for good."

"I hope," Max said.

Three days went by. Nothing happened. I wasn't exactly sure what to think, but I figured that if they were going to get us they would have done it by that point. Max agreed with me. She said we were probably in the clear. At last, we could finally relax.

On Wednesday, Max and I picked each other as partners for making a history diorama. We decided to work on it at my house right after school. We'd make the Indians out of clay and use my dad's shoe-shine chamois for a teepee.

On the way up my driveway, I decided to check the mail. Carefully, I opened the box. There were some catalogues and a bill from the telephone company. So far so good. That was, until I saw an envelope addressed to me.

"Oh, no," I gasped under my breath. I dropped my book bag on the ground and ripped open the envelope.

It looked a lot like the last one. The words were all cut out from different magazines and pasted on the paper. It read:

3 DAYS — THE BIRD STILL AIN'T TALKING. DELIVER THE RIGHT ONE OR YOU'LL WIND UP LIKE THE FIRST. NOON SATURDAY 6TH & SAMSON. ANY TRICKS AND . . .

Then they had pasted down a picture of chopped meat, and a yellow feather from the bird.

A chill rocketed up my spine. I knew that if we didn't cooperate this time they'd get us.

I could hardly look at Max when I said, "I guess we have no choice. We have to give them Pogo."

When we walked in the house my mom came downstairs.

"Hi, guys," she said. "Would you like an after-school snack?"

When Max said no my mom pretended to faint. "Well, Max, that's the first time you've ever refused a snack. Is something wrong?"

"Sort of," I said, "Max has the flu and doesn't feel like eating."

"Well, don't you think she should go home if she has the flu?"

"You're right," I said.

Max whispered that she was scared to walk home by herself. I walked her halfway and told her to run the rest of the way. Actually, I watched her all the way, then I ran back to my house. At this point it seemed like anything could happen.

10.
The Big Drop

Wednesday night was the worst. I couldn't keep my mind on anything. I could hardly eat or sleep. Max was the only person I could talk to about the situation.

By Thursday Max and I were flipping out. When the bell rang at recess, we met by the woods to try to get a plan together.

"Max, we don't have any choice," I said. "We have to give them Pogo."

"Well, what will we tell Mrs. Rice? If she comes home and finds Pogo missing, she'll probably call the police."

"Well," I said, "maybe we could find another parrot and stick it in Pogo's cage. Once I had a turtle that died. It was two months before I noticed my parents had put in a different turtle."

"Where are we going to find another parrot that says 'shut up' and 'you look marvelous'?"

"Yeah, you're right," I agreed. "Besides, Pogo looks like some kind of mutant with his cracked beak and bulging eyes. He'd probably be impossible to replace."

"Maybe we could say that we took him outside for some fresh air and he got away," Max said.

"Yeah," I agreed. "That sounds good. Then we could work and buy her a new one. Okay," I said, feeling a little better. "The next problem: How are we going to get Pogo to the drop-off spot on Saturday?"

"We're not calling Vinnie again," Max said firmly. "We're not going to pay limousine rates to ride around in that scum mobile. I'd rather walk."

"Max, we can't walk ten miles carrying a parrot. Besides, everyone would see us," I said. "We have to call Vinnie."

I think we both knew the answer.

So after school that day, I got off the bus with Max and we made the call.

I dialed and handed Max the phone as soon as Vinnie picked up. Max wanted to do the talking.

"Hi, Vinnie. This is Max, Robert's friend," she said. "Yes, Vinnie, it has everything to do with money. We'd like to arrange payment in full today as well as one free trip for 'frequent riders.'"

I couldn't believe my ears. She got that idea from an airline commercial. She was brilliant. I grabbed the phone.

"Hey, Vin, it's me, Rob. What do you think?"

Surprisingly, Vinnie was real nice. I didn't know why but he said, "Sure, I'd be glad to help you guys out again. What do you need to drop off this time?" he asked.

"Well," I said, "it's a parrot."

"Oh, a parrot? When?"

"On Saturday at noon. Fifth and Samson again."

"No problem. But first I'd really like to have a little meeting with the two of you. How about tomorrow after school? In the parking lot. I'll even give you a free ride home."

I realized then that he was up to something. I just wasn't sure what.

"Okay," I said and played along. "We'll see you tomorrow."

"He's going to do it, right?" Max asked.

"Yeah, but he wants to meet with us tomorrow. I think he's up to something."

"Maybe he's going to announce his engagement to that Carla girl. Or maybe she needs you to get her some new lipstick."

"Cut it out, Max."

By Friday afternoon, Max and I were total maniacs. When the school bell rang, we grabbed our stuff and ran out to the parking lot. Vinnie was already there.

We walked over to his car and climbed in the back. Vinnie turned around in his seat so he could look us right in the eye.

"Hi," I said and forced a smile.

"Hi, Vinnie," Max said. Then she smiled, too.

"Let's skip the formalities, kiddies. Call it intuition. I've got a nose for trouble. And I smell trouble. I know you two are up to something. Now, I figure it can't be too big because you're just little squirts. But it's something. And you're gonna tell me what. Now!"

Max looked at me. At this point I didn't know what to do. Neither one of us said a word.

"Okay, guys," Vinnie said. "If you don't talk, we're talking major consequences here. I hate to think about what they might be."

"Okay, Vinnie. I'll tell you. But you've got to promise not to tell anyone."

"Scouts' honor," Vinnie said, crossing his heart.

"Okay," I began, "well, Max and I answered this ad in the newspaper a few weeks ago. It said we could make five thousand dollars a month. So we met with the guys who put the ad in the paper. They gave us cookies to sell to people."

Max pinched me. I don't think she wanted me to go on.

"Anyway," I continued, "we were supposed to sell the cookies and report back about the people who bought them."

"Report back on what?" Vinnie asked.

"Well, on what kind of stuff they had in their houses. Anyway, these guys turned out to be crooks. They robbed one of our customers while we were visiting."

"Which customer?" Vinnie asked.

"Her name is Mrs. Adamsworth."

"Mrs. Adamsworth . . . Mrs. Adamsworth," he said and tried to recall where he had heard the name. Then it hit him. His eyes grew.

"Mrs. Adamsworth is that rich lady they talked about on the news last week. I remember. The job was botched because she sicked her dogs on them."

I nodded. "We were there, but she didn't want Max and me to get in the newspaper. That's why she didn't mention us."

Vinnie looked so excited I thought he was going to jump over the seat.

"Hey, you mean you guys were working with Lucky Louisano and Lousy Lloyd, the con artists?"

"Well, yeah, but we didn't know they were crooks."

"There's a ten-thousand-dollar reward out for catching them! Did you know that?"

"Yes," I said. "But they're dangerous. They've sent Max and me two blackmail notes."

"Blackmail?"

"See, I kind of tried to impress them when we first went for the job. I told them about our pet-sitting business and how we take care of this very valuable parrot."

"Which, of course, was a big fat lie," Max said, looking at me unhappily.

"Now, they're blackmailing us to get the parrot."

Vinnie got this wild look in his eyes.

"Don't you guys see the big opportunity here?" he said.

"What are you talking about?" I said. "If we don't cooperate they'll turn us into the police. Max and I signed a contract with them."

"Contract smontract! You guys are minors — under age — it isn't legal!"

I couldn't believe my ears. It was too good to be true.

"Listen up, guys," Vinnie said, putting a hand around each of our necks. "I've got a plan that's going to make all of us rich. See, we'll deliver the parrot all right. But then, when they go for the bird, we're going to pop out of the bushes and capture these crooks. They won't know what hit them!"

"Are you crazy?" Max said.

Vinnie didn't hear a word she said. He just kept talking. "Trust me. It's a piece of cake."

"We'll be national heroes," he continued. "And we'll get the reward money on top of it! I should take two-thirds because I thought it up. You and Max get the rest, minus what you owe me, of course."

"How are we going to capture them?" I asked.

"No problem. I have my black belt. And you took a karate lesson or two yourself, kiddo. We'll see what you're made of."

Somehow Max actually got excited. "I took a self-defense class once, but I don't know," she said, shaking her head.

"Vinnie, isn't this dangerous?" I asked.

"Of course it is," he replied. "That's what makes it fun."

11.
The Karate Kids

For the next two hours, Vinnie laid out the plan. He made me and Max repeat it a thousand times, so we wouldn't forget it, but we were more worried about *Vinnie* forgetting it.

That night I hardly slept. I just hoped Vinnie knew what he was doing. He told us to meet him in front of Mrs. Rice's house at 11:00 A.M. I pretended I slept until ten that morning.

Around ten-thirty I got up, got dressed, and went downstairs. My parents were outside in the backyard. I could hear them discussing weeds. I yelled hi and poured myself a bowl of Cap'n Crunch. Just then the doorbell rang. I opened the door. There was a woman standing there.

"Hi," the lady said. "Are your parents home?"

"Yes," I said. "Whom shall I say is here?" I definitely had never seen her before.

"Mrs. Walker. I'm from the school district counseling department. And you must be Robert?"

Holy smoke, I thought. I completely forgot about all that stuff I had told Mr. Gomez and Mr. Wellborn.

"No," I said. "I'm Ricky. Come on in. My parents are out in the backyard."

"Thank you," she said, walking through the house. I pointed to the back door. Then I ran out the front door.

This was all I needed on top of everything else! I ran to Mrs. Rice's and got there just as Vinnie did. Max had been waiting for both of us.

I took out the key from under the mat and the three of us went inside. For once, Pogo was quiet. I fed him and changed the newspaper in his cage. Then I oiled his beak for the last time. I felt really sad for Pogo. Max wrote out a note and put it in his cage. "Oil his beak once a day or it will crack more."

Max helped me put a blanket over the cage. Vinnie paced all over the kitchen.

"Hurry up, you guys. We need to go over the plan again," he said nervously.

"We know the plan, Vinnie," Max said. "We drive to Sixth and Samson. We get there fifteen minutes early. We put Pogo's cage under the Stop sign. Then we hide in the bushes."

"That's right," Vinnie said. "Then, when they go to get the bird, we pop out and take them by surprise. When they bend down to pick up the cage,

I'll karate chop the fat guy, and you two take down the other one. I'll say 'Put your hands behind your back and keep your mouths shut' and do a karate move or two. Just don't go chicken on me."

"We won't," I said. Max didn't say anything.

"I mean it. No mistakes," Vinnie said, opening the door. "Let's go."

Max and I carried Pogo's cage out to the car and put it between us on the backseat. Pogo must have been kind of upset because he kept saying "Shut up, shut up, you look marvelous, you look marvelous" over and over again.

When we got there, I looked at my watch. Eleven-fifty. Max and I got out of the car and put Pogo's cage under the Stop sign. Then Vinnie parked the car down the street. We all hid behind this big trash Dumpster near some bushes. We waited. I could tell Vinnie was nervous. He kept zipping and unzipping his leather jacket. Then things started to happen really fast.

Mr. Louie and Mr. Lloyd pulled up five minutes early. They ran over and picked up the cage and put it in the back of an old beat-up brown van. I didn't think they could move so quickly.

Just as they shut the back doors, Vinnie sprung into the Samurai fight stance and yelled, "Drop the cage or you're history."

At first Mr. Louie and Mr. Lloyd looked shocked. They both did as he said. But then I saw Mr. Louie wink at Mr. Lloyd. Max and I were still hiding even though we were supposed to have popped out. We were too scared to move.

Suddenly, Mr. Lloyd spun around and slammed Vinnie into a wrestling hold. Mr. Louie came over and put his face to Vinnie's and shook his head and pretended to do a little karate chop. "Who taught you karate? Grandma?" Mr. Louie said, laughing.

"Ain't this rich," he said. Then he looked at Vinnie and said, "Make my day!" Mr. Louie and Mr. Lloyd laughed like crazy.

I kept my eyes on Vinnie. I never thought I'd see him look so scared.

I was holding my breath. I prayed they didn't know Max and I were behind the Dumpster. Then I heard Mr. Louie belt out in his sing-song voice, "Now where are my two top salespeople hiding? Come out, come out, wherever you are."

Max and I grabbed each other's hands. Then we slowly came out and just stood there.

"Tie 'em up," Mr. Louie barked. Mr. Lloyd took a rope out of the van, tied our hands and feet really tight, and gagged us with one of Mr. Louie's smelly T-shirts. Next they made us get into the van. Pogo's cage was sitting between me and Max. Vinnie was lying right next to me. He looked very small when he was lying down, tied up.

Suddenly, I heard them start the engine. It seemed like it was really the end for all of us. Just as the van went in reverse, I heard a tapping sound on the side window.

Mr. Louie must have rolled down the window. It sounded like a policeman. I filled up with hope.

"I was just passing by and noticed that you're parked in a handicapped zone. Are you aware of that, sir? I'll need to see your license and registration."

"Oh yes, Mr. Officer, sir," I heard Mr. Louie say. Then I heard the glove compartment open and shut.

There was a long pause. Then I heard the cop say, "Looks like your registration expired three years ago. What do you have to say about that?"

Before Mr. Louie could answer, Pogo started squawking, "Shut up, shut up."

Then the cop said, "What did you say to me?"

"Oh, you see, sir, it was this gentleman here talking. He just got out of a mental hospital. Please don't take offense."

The cop wasn't buying it. He said, "Who do you think you're kidding?"

Then Pogo started chirping like crazy, "You look marvelous, you look marvelous, you look marvelous."

The cop sounded furious. "That's enough! Get out of the car, NOW!"

Next thing I knew, Mr. Louie put his foot on the gas pedal and floored it. He must have been going ninety miles an hour. The van was rocking like crazy. Pogo's cage was sliding from side to side, taking turns knocking Max and me in the head.

I heard Mr. Louie say, "Ha — Ha — the guy was on a horse. By the time he alerts a patrol car, we'll be a memory."

"What should we do with the kiddie cops back there?"

"Dump 'em," Mr. Lloyd answered.

"Do you think they'll talk?"

Of course they'll talk . . . if they're alive." Then he laughed this horrible laugh.

Pogo started yakking again so it was hard to hear the rest of what they were saying.

Next Mr. Lloyd asked, "What do you think we could get for the bird?"

"Five grand, tops. I've already got a guy that says he wants it."

Meanwhile, Max had been squirming like mad. Somehow, she had managed to get the gag off her mouth.

"Robert," she whispered, "what do you think they're going to do with us?"

I couldn't answer, but I was wondering the same thing.

After some time, we felt the van come to a stop. The crooks opened up the back doors to get us.

Max screamed as loud as she could, "Help! Help us! We're kidnapped." Mr. Louie quickly slapped his hand over Max's mouth. Then he tore another piece off his T-shirt and gagged her.

Worse, they put smelly old blankets over the three of us.

"Everyone will think they're just new customers for Jansen's Funeral Parlor," Mr. Louie said.

That's when I realized we must be back at 423 King Street.

One by one, they carried us upstairs with the blankets over us. I figured out we were in the room where we had our meetings.

"What do we do with 'em now?" Mr. Lloyd asked.

"I dunno. Maybe we should stick 'em in the closet. There's plenty of air in there. We'll be in Mexico before anyone finds them. Heh. Heh. Heh."

"I hope you're right. Hey, maybe we should take the big guy with us. That kid's got potential."

"Maybe we should take them all with us," Mr. Louie said.

"Are you crazy? Don't go soft on me, Louie. They'll be fine in there."

Then they stuck us inside the closet, and locked the door from the outside.

We could hear everything they said through the closet door.

Mr. Lloyd said, "Hey Lou, are you packed and ready to roll?"

"Yeah. But, by the way, where'd ya put that bag of gold coins?"

"Don't worry about it. You worry too much."

"You're not trying to hold out on me, are ya?" Mr. Louie asked.

Then their voices got really loud and they hollered at each other. Crash! I heard a table go over. Max and I stared at each other the whole time. Vinnie's eyes were closed, but he was whimpering like a baby.

Suddenly, the phone rang. And rang and rang. They argued about whether or not to answer.

Then Mr. Lloyd picked it up. "Arnie's Bar, Grill, and Funeral Parlor. You kill 'em, we chill 'em."

Mr. Louie must have grabbed the phone out of his hand. I heard him slam down the receiver.

"You numbskull!" Mr. Louie yelled. "What if it's the cops? They'll be stinkin' all over this place like mold on cheese."

"Let's get out of here." Then I heard some drawers slamming. I figured they were packing up the rest of their stuff.

Right before they left, I heard them put the key in our closet door.

The door opened and Mr. Louie took off Max's gag. He threatened that if she started to scream it would go right back on. Then he removed mine and Vinnie's, too.

None of us said a word. Mr. Louie left for a minute and then came back. He put a bowl of water on the floor. Then he put down a paper plate with some sliced pepperoni and a couple of squiggles of Cheese Whiz. He patted Max and me on the head and relocked the door.

"Ready?" Mr. Lloyd asked.

Mr. Louie replied. "Let's rock 'n' roll!"

One of them, tapped on the closet door and said, "So long, guys. Nice workin' with you. You should be gettin' your commission checks any day now."

Then they both laughed and the front door slammed.

All I thought about then was all the trouble I was going to be in. I couldn't decide if it was worse if they found us, or if they didn't.

Then everybody involved came into my mind at once. Mr. O'Hara, Mrs. Adamsworth, my mom and dad. Even Max. I was the one who got us into this whole mess.

I promised myself that if I ever got out of that closet I would never do something like this again.

12.
Hard Knocks

I was afraid to speak until I was sure they weren't coming back. I waited for a long time before I whispered to Max, "I'm sorry I got us into all this. It's really my fault."

"Well," Max said, "how were you supposed to know they were crooks?"

"I don't know," I said.

"Hey, they fooled me, too."

Somehow that made me feel a little better.

"How long do you think we've been in here? How long do you think it will be before anyone finds us?" Vinnie whined.

"I don't know," I said. "Maybe they'll never find us. Maybe it will take twenty years."

Vinnie started to cry. "I've been doing a lot of thinking while I've been shut up in here. There's nothing else to do. Anyway, if we ever get out of here alive, I'm gonna forget all about the dough you owe me."

Then Max started to cry. We all cried.

I was hot. I was miserable. My legs ached. I would have done anything to be home safe in my bed.

It seemed like hours and hours went by. I worried we'd run out of air. Then, something happened. It was like a miracle.

"Hey, listen," I said. "I heard something! Like a hard knock!"

We waited for another sound.

"Yes," I screamed. "Someone's out there! Someone's out there!"

"Wait," Vinnie said. "What if it's those crooks? Maybe they decided to come back and kill us."

We all stayed real quiet. Then I heard it again. *K-bang. K-bang.* It sounded as if someone was trying to kick in the door.

Then it hit me. "Vinnie," I screamed. "If it were Mr. Louie or Mr. Lloyd, they'd have a key."

Then we all started screaming our heads off.

"Help! Help! We're in here! We're in the closet!"

Bam! Bam! I heard a loud crash. The door must have smashed to the floor.

"We're in the closet!" I yelled. "Over here, over here."

I heard my mother yelling.

"The closet — my baby's in the closet."

Someone tried to turn the doorknob.

"We'll have to break the lock. Are you kids all right in there?"

"Yeah," I answered.

"A little hungry," Max said.

"Okay, I'm Detective Green," the man said. "We're going to break the lock off. Move as far away as possible from the door."

Our hands and feet were still tied up so we kind of moved around like inchworms. The closet was small, so there wasn't much room to move back.

"Ready?" the detective yelled.

"Ready," we yelled.

Then we heard this hack, hack sound and the door sprung open.

I looked up and there was everybody — my mom, my dad, Mr. Laramax, Mrs. Laramax, a detective, a policeman, and two guys in suits.

The policeman pulled us to our feet. My mother kissed me all over. Then my dad untied my hands and feet. Mrs. Laramax did the same for Max and Vinnie. My dad even had tears in his eyes. He gave me a long, hard hug.

The fun part didn't last long, however. Once everyone saw we were okay, the questions began to fly.

"My name is Detective Green. We need some answers. And fast."

"Yes, sir," I said.

"We know who these characters are. What we

need to know from you is a description of the car they're driving, and where they're headed."

"They're driving a beat-up old brown van. I think it's a Ford," I said.

"I wouldn't call it beat-up," Vinnie said.

"They're headed for Mexico," Max said. "I overheard them."

"How long would you estimate it's been since they took off?"

"I don't know — it's been about three or four hours since they put us in here."

"Okay, great, I'm going to radio that in right now."

Detective Green put the radio control up to his mouth and said: "This is Detective Green calling Highway Patrol. The suspects are driving a brown Ford van. Pretty beat-up. They're headed to Mexico. They've been on the road approximately three hours."

Then the other voice said, "This is unit four, I read you loud and clear. Old brown Ford van. Over."

The whole time my dad and Mr. Laramax were pacing up and down the room. I couldn't even look at my mom. I tried to keep my eyes on the detective as long as possible.

"How did you even know we were here?" I asked my dad.

"Your mom found the blackmail note this morn-

109

ing when she went to wash your jeans. She called Max's house and her mom had just discovered the address scribbled on a piece of paper. Then your mother called the police."

"By the time we got to the scene, the crooks had left." Detective Green said. "But the patrol officer got the license and we traced it here."

My mother sobbed again when she heard that.

"But the real question is, how did you kids get involved with these guys?" Mr. Laramax asked, looking right at me.

Before we could answer, Detective Green was signaled on the radio.

The voice said, "Detective Green, this is unit five. The suspects in question have just been spotted. They're parked outside a Pizza Hut in Centerville. We're moving in on them. Over."

Vinnie's eyes lit up. "You got them. Great. I guess we'll be getting some reward money, huh?"

"That's not my decision to make," Detective Green said, "but I have a feeling you didn't apprehend them exactly the way the police had in mind."

Detective Green turned to Max and me and said, "You kids have been very, very lucky. Now please explain how you got mixed up in all this."

I decided to tell the truth. "We answered an ad in the paper to make a lot of money selling these Cash-in-Advance Cookies. But the crooks just used us so they could steal people's stuff."

"Is there anyone else you sold cookies to?" Detective Green asked.

"No," I said.

"Thank goodness," Max added.

"Next, they blackmailed us to get Pogo. For some reason they thought he was worth a lot of money." Max just looked at me.

"Well, you kids have been through quite a bit. We're going to let you go home now. We might have to do some more questioning later."

Detective Green handed my dad and Max's dad a business card. Then we all cleared out.

Max and I didn't get a chance to say much to each other. Vinnie came in the car with me and my parents.

One of the policemen drove me, Vinnie, and my mom and dad home. I was glad. I figured my dad wouldn't yell at me in front of a stranger. Boy, was I wrong!

The next day, the whole world had heard about what happened. Vinnie, Max, and me made the front page of the *Thornton Daily News*. Both editions. It was a good picture of me and Max, but Vinnie looked a little stupid the way he was smiling.

That Monday morning my dad decided to drive me to school. I figured he just wanted another chance to yell at me but actually he was pretty nice.

When I walked into my classroom, everybody

turned around and stared. Max didn't look up. I didn't know what to do so I just waved. Then I walked over to my desk and pulled out my math book. I had a feeling Mrs. Hunt was looking in my direction so I looked up. She pointed her finger at me. Then she motioned for me to come up.

When I got in front of her desk, she made me walk around to the side.

"Robert," she said, kind of low.

"Yes?" I said, waiting.

"'Oh, what a tangled web we weave, when first we practice to deceive.'"

I just stared at her. I thought she was talking about lying but I wasn't sure. Next she did something pretty horrible. She pulled me close and hugged me. Then she kissed me on the forehead.

The room got completely silent. Then, just like that, she turned mean again. Really loud she said, "Now go back and finish that math or you're staying with me after school." Then she narrowed her eyes like a snake. "For the rest of the week," she added.

The Iron Lung was back. I was so relieved.

I know Max was terrified that she was next because she immediately raised her hand to go to the bathroom.

But then something worse happened. As soon as the lunch bell rang, I hurried into the cafeteria and put down my lunch bag at our usual spot. Then I put my milk container on Max's chair because whoever got there first always saved the seat. But Max never showed.

I looked all around the room. That's when I spotted her. She was three tables away sitting next to Jeff. He was eating his sandwich and looking at her like she was some kind of hero. It was pretty disgusting. I didn't mind eating alone that day, but I hoped it wasn't going to be a habit with her. I wasn't jealous or anything.

"Hey, Max," I yelled across the lunchroom. "Meet me in front of the woods at oh-four hundred hours." That was our secret code for "right away." It was no use. She was too busy signing autographs.

So then I figured it was as good a time as any to do what I had promised my parents — apologize to Mr. Wellborn. I started walking toward his office thinking up something to say. Mostly I just wished he wasn't going to be there. My palms were all sweaty by the time I knocked on his door. He was there.

"Robert, come in," he said. I couldn't believe it but he smiled at me. He didn't say anything more so I figured I'd better start talking.

"Mr. Wellborn, I just wanted to say I'm sorry about kind of making everybody think my parents were, you know . . ." I couldn't think of what else to say, so I cleared my throat. Then I wiped my sweaty hands on my pants and started over.

"I mean, I'm sorry that I lied about my parents

getting a divorce to Mr. Gomez and then by the time I got to you I got carried away. Things kind of got out of hand. Do you know what I mean?" I don't think I took a breath the whole time. I was really nervous.

Mr. Wellborn stood up. He had on another one of those peppy outfits. He walked over and stuck out his hand. I shook it.

"Apology accepted," he said. "I'm sure that little escapade taught you more than I ever could with words."

"Yeah," I agreed. Then the bell rang, so I said good-bye and headed back to my classroom.

That night I also had to call Mrs. Walker, the counselor, and tell her I was sorry. She said she'd be interested in meeting me sometime.

Oh, and that night Mrs. Rice called to tell me Pogo was fine and we still had the job. Can you believe it! She also said Pogo had picked up some really bad habits. Now he burps a lot and says "That's rich, that's rich!" and then laughs like crazy. I told her we'd try to get him to stop.

The next day, Max and I finally got a chance to talk about things. That's when we decided to go visit Mrs. Adamsworth after school.

It was a really fun visit. Mrs. Adamsworth was so happy to see us. She said she would whack us with her cane if we ever got mixed up in another crazy scheme like that again. Then she said if we wanted to make some money she had plenty of work around her place that needed to be done.

We told her we would try to come by on Saturday. We didn't know until that night that we had already been employed elsewhere.

You see, my dad and Max's dad got together and decided that Max and I needed to learn that get-rich-quick schemes never work.

Translation: Max and I had to shovel horse manure out of Mr. O'Hara's barn for a whole month! For free! After that he was allowed to pay us fifty cents a wheelbarrow again.

Finally, our days of shoveling for free were over. When I got home, I took a shower, and went to my room. I lay on my bed and thought about Mr. Louie and Mr. Lloyd. I thought about writing them a letter and sending it to their jail cell. I just wanted them to know that I had a feeling they were crooks all along. I was about to get some paper when my dad called me from downstairs.

"Hey, Robert," he yelled, "come outside in the backyard as soon as you're dressed. I want to show you something."

"Okay, Dad," I yelled back. Oh, great, I thought to myself. He probably had some more work waiting for me. Maybe he didn't believe I had learned my lesson.

So anyway, I put on my jeans and T-shirt and

headed for the backyard. When I walked through the kitchen, my mom gave me one of those sweet looks. Uh-oh, I thought. It must be something really horrible. I opened the back door and walked out into the yard.

I looked around, but I didn't see him. "Dad," I yelled. "I'm here." But there was no answer.

"Oh, Dad," I yelled again. "You wanted to see me?" Still no answer.

I was just about to go back inside when I felt this blast of water on my back. I turned around and there was my dad. I couldn't believe my eyes. He was holding a brand new Super Soaker 2000 in his hands!

He squirted me again, so I chased him around the yard. Then my mom came running out of the house and he squirted her, too. We were all soaked and laughing our heads off.

"Wow," I said when my dad handed it over. "Thanks a lot." I gave both of my parents a hug. I guess you could say it was just my lucky day.